Mountain Daddy Does it Better

A Romantic Novel About a Daddy Dom Who Trains His Baby Girl in the DDLG and ABDL kink

By Tina Moore

Table of Contents

Chapter 1

Lana's hybrid skidded wildly in the mud as she gripped the wheel so hard that her knuckles turned white, forcefully guiding the sedan back onto the road. According to the map, she was only twenty minutes away from the cabin which she had rented for the summer in a secluded spot in the Georgia mountains. If the rain kept up like it was, then it was going to be a whole lot longer before she was finally out of this car.

She had driven straight here from Orlando, Florida, opting to travel in one long marathon session rather than breaking it up into two shorter trips. It was a long, boring drive through mostly farmland but everything was going as planned until this thunderstorm came seemingly out of nowhere. As she squinted through the dark, trying desperately to stay on the road, she was beginning to wonder if that had been a bad plan. Of course, originally the plan had involved a tag-team effort.

She wasn't supposed to be taking this trip alone. Her boyfriend Mike had convinced her that they should take advantage of the two-month vacation that came with being an office lady at a local school by renting a cabin and escaping the heat and humidity of the Florida summer. He was a writer, after all, and could work from anywhere, he had argued. He had painted a lovely picture of the two of them tucked away in their little love nest in the mountains, far away from the problems of real life. Lana agreed, eager for a change in scenery, and booked the cabin. The entire trip was on her credit card, of course. He was always suggesting things to do and then asking her to pay for them, saying that writing didn't pay very well, as if teaching were some lucrative career that kept her rolling in money.

Then, only a week before they were supposed to leave, he dumped her out of the blue. He said that he had met a model who was in town from Miami and that they were in love and were going to move in together. Lana had cried so many tears over that man, and she was sure she would cry many more. Her instinct had been to pay the cancellation fee and stay home to tend to her broken heart, but her friend Barb had convinced her that a change in scenery would do her good.

"Forget about that cheating bastard for a few weeks. See if you can find a handsome, rugged mountain man to take your mind off things," she had said. Lana had blushed at that last suggestion but had to admit that the idea had merit. Why should she sit around feeling sorry for herself while he was off with having the time of his life? She should look at this as dodging a bullet. Better to find out now that Mike was disloyal rather than years down the road. She wiped a tear from her eye.

Lana's car started picking up speed as she went down a sharp incline. She tapped her brakes, but the mud was too slippery. She was going too fast when she saw the downed branch, and it was too late to avoid it. It clattered underneath the car, tangling itself in the tires. She slid into the ditch, and that was the last thing she remembered for a long time.

***

Micah's oversized tires were having some trouble getting through the mud. It took a really bad storm to bog down his truck, and this one was a real doozy. With a muttered curse, he had pretty much decided to head back to his hunting cabin, unwilling to fight this chaos just for some beer. Just then, he saw headlights off in the bushes. His heart leaped into his throat at the thought of someone hurt or worse, and he brought his truck to a stop, shifting it into park and putting on his hazards. He hadn't thought to bring an umbrella, it had hardly been sprinkling when he left, and he was soaked immediately upon stepping out onto the muddy dirt road.

He went slowly, cautiously toward the crashed

vehicle, hoping it wouldn't be something beyond his limited ability to help. An ambulance would have a hell of a time getting up here in these conditions. With a shaky hand, he pushed some branches aside and pulled the driver's side door open. It was dented, but it still opened without too much of a fight. Hunched over the steering wheel was a young woman with dark hair. He couldn't tell much else about her, including her health status.

"Ma'am," he said softly, not wanting to startle her. "Are you ok?" There was no response at first, so he nudged her arm gently. She groaned at that, and he sighed in relief. At least she was alive.

"Ma'am, can you move?" She groaned again and shifted her head. She wasn't totally awake yet, but she seemed to be coming around a little. "We need to get you to a doctor. I'm going to help you out of the car now. We can take my truck into town." Her eyes fluttered open, but she couldn't seem to be able to focus on anything, and they quickly closed again. He put his arm gingerly around her waist, worried about overstepping his bounds or injuring her further.

"Let me know if I hurt you, ma'am," he said as he slid his arms underneath her small frame and began to lift her out. She didn't make any noises, only wrapped her arms around his neck, tight as anything.

She's a strong little thing, he thought. *That's a good sign.* He held her close to him, trying to shield her from the rain as much as possible as he carried her to the passenger side of his truck, laying her on the front seat as gently as he could. As he came around to the driver's side, he got a better look at the spot where she had skidded off the road. It was going to be a challenge making it over the deep ruts her spinning tires had made in the road, but it was doable. He got in, grateful to be out of the deluge once again.

"Are you ok, little one?" he muttered, not really expecting a response from the unconscious woman. He put his hand on her forehead, brushing away the wet hair that was stuck to her skin. By the light of the dashboard, he could tell that she was pretty, brownish hair and delicate features. She seemed tiny compared to him, and her petite frame was shivering from head to toe. He cranked up the heat, cursing himself for not having a blanket or spare jacket in the truck. But how could he have known? It was the middle of May, after all.

"Don't worry," he said, putting the truck into drive. "We'll have you fixed up in no time at all." Despite his false optimism, it was slow going. The roads seemed to be getting worse by the minute. He had only made it a little more than half a mile when he heard the local radio station announce that the main road into town was washed out due to a mudslide and that several other roads into town were being closed as well as a precautionary measure. All residents were advised to stay in their homes until further notice. Micah looked at the little bundle on the seat next to him, his heart sinking more and more by the second. He knew his way around a first aid kit well enough, but she needed more than that. Under the circumstances, however, it might be a while before she could get the care she needed. He hated feeling so helpless. His protective instincts were in overdrive, but he didn't have many options. For the moment, the only thing he could do was to take her somewhere warm and comfortable and call a doctor for advice, then wait for the roads to clear. He slapped the steering wheel, frustrated as hell. After a moment of fuming, he put the truck into reverse and made his way back to his hunting cabin. There was nothing for it. He would just have to take care of her by himself.

Chapter 2

When Lana woke up, she stretched her arms and yawned before suddenly freezing. The last thing she remembered, she had been driving in the rain. How did she get to this comfortable, dry place? She opened her eyes to see that she was on a small bed, covered by a thick blanket. It was a small room that was sparsely decorated. Her hair was damp, as were her clothes.

"Hello?" she called out, feeling disoriented and more than a little dizzy. "Anyone home?" A man hurriedly came into the room, a huge mountain of a man, and waved awkwardly at her from the doorway. He didn't look familiar to her, and she squinted at him, more confused than ever.

"Hello, ma'am," he said. "Sorry to just whisk you away like that. You were hurt, and I couldn't just leave you. Do you remember crashing your car?" She shook her head, but just as she did, the memories came flooding back to her. The branch in the road, the screech of metal on wood, the sudden pain. "Oh, yeah," she said vaguely, then lay back down on the pillow. "It was raining."

"Right. It's still raining, and the roads are washed out. I called the hospital and told them what happened. They said the best thing for you right now is rest. Are you hurt, are you in any pain?" She did a careful scan of her body, noticing for the first time a throbbing ache in her wrist.

"My wrist hurts," she said through parched lips. "And I'm dizzy. And thirsty." His brow wrinkled, and she noticed that once you got past his size, he was a very handsome man. He had black hair, beautiful sea-green eyes, and a chiseled jawline. He seemed a few years older than her, early thirties perhaps. His frame was both tall and broad, but his form seemed toned, well-muscled. Even in her compromised position, she couldn't help but notice that he was wearing the hell out of those blue jeans.

"Wait right here," he said. "I'll get you water and an ice pack." He was gone for several minutes, the sound of running water coming from the next room. It occurred to her that he could be a psychopath and that she could be trapped in some kind of reverse Misery scenario. However, as he came back into the room with a pink sippy cup in one hand and a bag of frozen peas in the other, it did seem rather unlikely. Even if it were the case, she was in very little position to do anything about it. He put the peas on the bedside table and brought the sippy cup over to the bed. Lana tried to sit up to drink, but he stopped her.

"The doctor said to rest, so that's what you're going to do, little one." He put his giant paw of a hand under her head and lifted it so that she could drink. "All of it," he prompted when she tried to lay her head back down again. His voice was firm and authoritative, and Lana could feel herself responding to his dominant energy. It put her at ease but also excited her in a way that caught her off guard. She drank all the water down and licked her lips with a satisfied sigh as her body soaked in the hydration. Already, she felt a little more energetic and a little more alert. He picked up the peas and held them against her swollen wrist. She winced at the pressure but was grateful to feel the coolness against her fevered flesh. Hopefully, it would numb the pain entirely after a while.

"Who are you?" she asked and then blushed. "Sorry if that sounded rude. I meant, what is your name?" He chuckled and nodded.

"Not rude at all, ma'am. I reckon you have a right to ask as many questions as you would like. My name is Micah, and this is my hunting cabin. I like to come here a couple of times a year, you know, get away from it all. I was going to make a quick beer run when all hell let loose. I saw you in the ditch and tried to get you to the hospital, but it was already too late, the mudslide had already blocked the roads. I'm afraid we're stuck here until morning at least. Where were you headed? Is there someone I can call?" She shook her head and instantly regretted it as the world began to spin even faster. Maybe it would be better to use her words.

"There's no one to call, just some friends back home. I'm here on vacation. The agent was going to leave the key in a dropbox for me since I was coming into town so late," she said.

"Oh, ok. So you're here alone, then?" She sighed and bit her lip before answering.

"Yes, I was supposed to be coming here with my boyfriend but, well," She trailed off, looking very sad.

"But you guys are no longer together," he guessed, nodding sympathetically. "I've been there. What about your family?"

"My Mom passed a few years back, and I never met my Dad. No siblings. It was just my Mom and I, and now it's just me."

"Oh boy, I just keep asking all the wrong questions, don't I? I promise I'm not trying to make you relive these terrible things on purpose." Lana got a wry chuckle out of that.

"It's not your fault that I'm having an

unlucky streak lately. Don't worry about it," she replied. He scratched his head and looked abashed. It was a good look on him.

"Well, anyway, the doc said you should rest. Hold tight for just a second, Lana." He grabbed the sippy cup and went back to the kitchen to refill it, rifling around in the cabinets before returning. In his comfortingly oversized hand were two blue pills. *He's so big. It's a bit like being nursed by a Wookie,* she thought to herself, stifling a giggle. It would be rude to laugh in the man's face when he was being so kind to her.

"These will help you sleep and help with the pain," he said. "Open." She obeyed without thinking, again responding to his dominant aura and authoritative tone. He placed the pills on her moist, pink tongue, his fingers grazing her lips as he did so, then held the sippy cup up for her to wash them down with.

"There," he said as she swallowed them. "How is your wrist feeling?"

"Numb," she said. "Better." He took the pack

of frozen peas off her wrist and examined it closely. As he studied her wrist, she was surprised at how gentle such a large man could be, his fingers just barely applying pressure as he held her arm. He ran his fingertips lightly over her skin and nodded.

"Doesn't seem to be broken but we can't know for sure until we can get it x rayed. Try to get some sleep. I'll be in to check on you again in a few hours." He got up to go, taking the package of peas with him.

"Wait, how did you know my name," she asked, suddenly realizing that she had never given it to him.

"Oh," he said, scratching his head again. It seemed to be a nervous tick of his. "I had to look at your I.D. for the hospital. They wanted your name and some other info. Sorry, I wasn't trying to be a creep, I promise."

"It's okay," she said sleepily. "You were just trying to help." As she closed her eyes again, he took a few more steps toward the door, treading as softly as he could.

"Micah," She called out weakly, already drifting back off to sleep. He hesitated in the doorway.

"Yes, lit - Lana?"

"Thank you for taking care of me."

"You're very welcome. Sweet dreams," he said quietly. He turned off the lights and closed the door quietly behind him.

Chapter 3

Lana woke up to the feeling of Micah's hand on her forehead. His fingers sought out the pulse on her neck and paused there, counting the beats. Her eyes fluttered open, and he smiled at her.

He has such a nice smile, she thought groggily. She felt caught in his gaze like a deer caught in the headlights, his green eyes twinkling in the low light.

"How are you feeling?" he asked, his voice full of concern.

"Hot," she said, suddenly noticing that she was drenched with sweat. She tried to kick off the blankets, but the minute that she moved, she froze. In her sleep, she had wet her diaper. The synthetic material was sticky and moist between her legs and, as she moved, the smell of urine wafted up. She cringed, hoping that he hadn't noticed.

"What's wrong?" asked Micah, sensing the sudden tension in the air. Lana felt her entire being burning with embarrassment. When she didn't answer right away, Micah's voice grew slightly panicked. "Are you hurt? Lana? Talk to me!"

"No, I'm not hurt, I just need to get to the bathroom." She knew that she was blushing, but she hoped he would just chalk that up to modesty. He was visibly relieved, his shoulders sagging as he let out a small sigh.

"Oh, of course! Sit up slowly, and I'll help you get down the hall. It isn't far." He put his hands under her shoulders and lifted her up. A wave of dizziness washed over her, and he held her up as she took a moment to get used to sitting upright. Eventually, the dizziness faded, and she was able to swing her legs off the edge of the bed and gingerly put her weight on her feet. As soon as she did, shooting pain in her ankle made her cry out and she sat back down on the bed hard, instinctively clutching at it.

"What happened?" asked Micah. His hands flew to the ankle she was grasping, wrapping his hands gently around hers. "Is your ankle broken? Let me see." He gently removed her hands, examining the swollen joint, shaking his head with dismay.

"You won't be walking on this anytime soon, I'm afraid. It's very swollen. If you want, I can carry you and help you onto the toilet." She blushed furiously, knowing that would include pulling down her pants and discovering her secret. It was unavoidable. It would seem. She had to get out of this wet diaper, and for that, she would require his help. Still, she had managed to keep this tendency of hers a secret for this long and part of her had hoped that no one would ever find out, even if it were a stranger who she would likely never see again.

"Hey, there's no need to be embarrassed," he said, his voice gentle and warm. His kindness only made her feel more ashamed. This nice, handsome man was about to learn what she had kept from so many boyfriends all these years.

"No, you don't understand," she said, avoiding his gaze. "I don't need to go to the bathroom because ... I already did." She buried her face in the pillow, wishing the earth would open up and swallow her whole. Micah didn't say anything for a long time, which made her nervous. Was he mad? Stifling laughter in an effort to be polite? Trying to find the quickest way out of there? She wanted to know but didn't have the courage to lift her head and look him in the eye.

"So, do you need me to help you get cleaned up?" he said, finally. There was no ridicule in his voice, nor was there anger. She still couldn't look at him, but she answered him, her words slightly muffled by the pillow.

"I'm sorry." She was on the verge of tears, and her voice cracked. Micah put his hand on her chin, gently pulling her face towards him.

"Look at me. I can't hear you when you have your face in the pillow like that." She turned her face towards him, her eyes cast downward.

She would never be able to look him in the eye again; she was certain of it.

"I said, I'm sorry." Her lower lip trembled, and the tears threatened to flood out but she just barely hold them back. Micah's thumb gently circled her chin, and he sighed.

"I told you to look at me," he said firmly. She obeyed, unable to resist his dominant tone. Despite her deep shame, she managed to look at him. "There is nothing to be sorry about. You are hurt, and you need help. I'm here and capable of giving you that help. If the tables were turned, wouldn't you help me?" She nodded, staring at him with big watery eyes. The effect that he had on her was stunning. She felt like she had been hit by a truck. A big, sexy, dominant truck.

"See? Now, I'm going to take your pants off, ok? I'll be as gentle as I can be, but I need you to let me know if I hurt your ankle or anything else." She blushed but tried to be brave. "Ok, I will." He nodded and moved to unbutton her jeans but hesitated, his fingers lingering over the clasp. He cleared his throat and shifted his weight slightly, and Lana was sure that he was more uncomfortable than he was letting on. She picked up the pillow and covered her face with it, hiding from her humiliation. A second later, Micah picked up the pillow and looked at her quizzically. Just when she thought that she couldn't get any more mortified, here he was looking at her like she was a crazy person.

"What are you doing?" he asked.

"I ... I'm still embarrassed." Her face burned, and she knew that she was blushing deeply.

"I know, little one," he said gently. She gasped quietly at the term of endearment but brushed it off, ignoring the heat it made her feel inside. Everyone probably seemed little to Micah. It probably didn't have the same significance to him as it did to her. "But it has to be done. I promise I won't laugh or make fun. Ok?" She nodded, feeling a little bit better. He smiled tentatively and unbuttoned her pants. He tugged at the waistband and froze when he saw that instead of underwear, she was wearing a diaper. She had no idea what to say as he stared down at her, his jaw slack with surprise.

"I'm sorry," she finally said, desperate to fill the awkward silence. He shook his head slightly, coming back to the present.

"No, don't be," he said, clearing his throat again. "It's a good thing you had this on, actually." He pulled her pants the rest of the way down, gently and slowly. She winced slightly as he brought the pants over her swollen ankle, but the pain was minuscule compared to her embarrassment.

"Do you have a medical condition?" he asked, and she could tell that he was fighting to keep his voice conversational. She appreciated the effort, amazed once again at his kindness towards her. "I'm sorry if that was a rude question, I just need to call the doc back if that's the case." She blushed and covered her face with her hands, groaning. It was tempting to use a fictional illness as an excuse, but she didn't want to lie to him.

"No, that's the worst part of all of this. I just like wearing them. I was feeling sorry for myself about the breakup, and so I wanted to wear one on my vacation to make myself feel better. I don't usually use them, I just." She trailed off and started crying. Hearing the words out loud was just too much, and she couldn't hold them back anymore. He perched next to her on the bed, taking up what little space was left and lifted her up, folding her in his arms. They felt so good around her, so strong and safe.

"There, there," he said soothingly. "It's ok, little one. Let it all out." He rocked her back and forth, holding her until she stopped crying and rubbing her back lightly to calm her. Eventually, her sniffles and sobs stopped. She pulled back slightly to see that she had soaked the front of Micah's shirt and was doubly mortified.

"Don't worry about it," he said gruffly, following her horrified gaze to the wet stain on his chest. He pulled a tissue from a box on the nightstand and gently wiped her face with it. He held it up to her nose and commanded her to blow. "Listen to me, Lana. No, don't look away. Look at me and listen. Don't ever be ashamed of being a little, ok? There is nothing wrong with you. There is no reason to be ashamed. Ok?" As the meaning behind his words began to sink in, it was her turn to stare at him in slack-jawed amazement.

"You know what a little is?!" He gently laughed at her astonishment. She would have felt embarrassed, but she somehow sensed that it wasn't mockery but rather a kind of admiration that had him so tickled.

"I do. I'm a Daddy Dom. Or weren't you wondering why I had a little pink sippy cup and no kids?"

"Well, no, actually. I - " She was at a loss. The odds of two people with the same sort of secret running into each other so far away from civilization were astounding.

"I happen to have some diapers and other things left behind by, a former companion of mine.

I could go get them if you like."

"Um, yeah, actually. That sounds really nice. If you don't mind sharing, that is." He smiled and lowered her back onto the bed, pulling the covers onto her legs. She couldn't help but notice how his hand lingered a bit on her thigh as he smoothed the covers down. Just that small amount of contact from him was enough to make her shiver all over.

"Not at all. Sit tight," he said with a wink and left the room. Her heart pounded as she waited for his return. She had never actually someone else that shared her preferences before. Not in real life, anyway. She had met a few friends online, but this was a whole new experience! This could actually be something. She had already been attracted to him before this revelation. His rugged, mountain man vibe was hard not to like after all. But she hadn't really given him that much thought since she probably wouldn't see him again after he took her to the hospital. Now, she suddenly felt nervous and excited. A real-life Daddy! The warm feeling she had gotten in her tummy was growing stronger. And lower. She blushed, embarrassed by her own body's reaction to a man she hardly knew. *Don't get ahead of yourself, Lana.*

He returned with a diaper bag and a stuffed bunny rabbit. She grinned when she saw the rabbit and forgot to be nervous for a moment. Stuffies were a huge source of comfort for her, and she had been secretly longing for hers, which had gotten left behind in her car. She had only brought two along for the trip, but they were her favorites, and she'd had them for years.

"I thought you might like to make a new friend," Micah said.

"Oh, I would! What's his name?"

"Well, as a matter of fact, he just told me the other day that he didn't like his old name anymore, can you believe that? Said he wasn't going to answer to it anymore. I think you should give him a new name. What do you think?" She giggled, her mood steadily improving as her crush on him got just a little bit bigger.

"Hmm. I think he looks like a Bernard," she

said after a moment's consideration. He held the bunny up to his ear, pretended to listen, then nodded.

"Bernard says he likes that." He gave her the stuffed bunny, and she held it close. A wave of comfort and relaxation came over her as she could feel herself enter her little space. The best part was, she didn't have to hide it around her new friend. She could openly be little and not have to worry. It was liberating.

He pulled a fresh diaper from the bag as well as some wipes and powder. Her eyes went wide, and she remembered to be nervous again. He pulled the covers back, and she couldn't help but notice the way his eyes lingered over her puffy diaper. She wondered what he was thinking but was too shy to ask.

"Have you ever been changed by anybody before?" he asked, his voice low and silky.

"No, I usually just do it myself."

"Well, lie back and relax, sweetie. Let me take care of you." His voice was so gentle. She found herself relaxing against the pillows and letting her knees fall open He loosened her diaper and began pulling it down. "Lift your hips. There's a good girl." His praise made her glow with pride. He pulled the diaper off, bundled it up, and put it in the trash. He kept his eyes averted to her exposed nakedness, pulling a wipe from the pack and draping it over her private area before using it to clean her up. It felt nice against her skin, cool and soft, and it was very hard not to think about how there was only a thin piece of cloth between them. Her face grew hot as she imagined him touching her down there for real. He tossed the wipe in the trash and pulled a new diaper from the pack, scooting it under her bottom. With a quick sprinkle of powder, he had her fastened back up in a flash. He pulled a bottle of hand sanitizer out of the bag and gave his hands a quick once over. He pulled the cover back over her and sat beside her, stroking her hair tenderly. His hands still had a lingering smell of alcohol, but she found that she didn't mind.

"See, that wasn't so bad, was it?" She smiled up at him, clutching Bernard tightly to her chest.

"No, that wasn't bad at all. It was really nice, actually." He returned her smile and brought his hand down to her cheek, stroking it lightly. She closed her eyes and nuzzled her face into his hand, beginning to feel the pull of the sleeping pills once again.

"How is your ankle feeling?"

"It still hurts," she said drowsily. "But I'm fine."

"We had better put some ice on it," she heard him say and felt him get up from the bed. In his brief absence, she drifted off to sleep again but woke up with a start when the frozen peas touched her inflamed ankle. "I'm sorry, little one. Go back to sleep."

"But it's cold," she whined and clutched Bernard tighter.

"I know it is, sweet girl. Just close your eyes, you'll forget all about it soon enough." He stroked her hair as he spoke, and her eyes fluttered closed.

As he petted her hair, he began humming a lullaby, and within minutes, her breath was coming slow and even. Micah tiptoed out of the room to let her rest.

Chapter 4

When Lana woke up again, it was morning. Well, almost morning. The first golden rays of dawn were just beginning to break through the grey night. She smelled the pungent odor of coffee wafting in from the next room and sat up excitedly.

"Micah?" she called out, wanting to let him know that she was awake. She sat up, searching for her pants which were on the floor near the door. As she put her foot tentatively on the floor, she heard him call to her from the kitchen.

"Hey! I thought the coffee might wake you up. How do you take yours?"

"Cream and sugar, please," she yelled back and tried her weight on her injured ankle. It hurt too much to walk on, so she decided to try hopping on one foot over to her pants. It went pretty well for about three and a half hops before she fell to the floor with a crash. She landed badly on her already injured wrist and yelped in pain. Micah came bursting into the room seconds later and rushed over to where she was lying on the floor, clutching her arm to her chest.

"What happened? What were you doing?" She pointed weakly to her pants, suddenly painfully aware that she had only a diaper and a t-shirt on and probably looked completely ridiculous sprawled out on the carpet. He looked at her with a combination of anger and concern on his handsome face. "Why didn't you call me?!" Before she could even answer, he had scooped her up from the floor and carried her as though she weighed nothing at all over to the bed. His brow was furrowed with concern as he studied her injured wrist for a moment before growling in frustration.

"I don't even know what I'm looking at!" He ran his hands through his shiny black hair in frustration. "The sheriff said the roads won't be cleared for another hour or so. You need a doctor now!"

"It's ok," she said, trying to calm him down. It was sweet that he was so concerned for her, but it was making her feel a tad guilty. She should have known better, should have just waited on him to help her get dressed. "I just jostled it a bit. Honestly, it's fine." He didn't look convinced, however, and looked at her with a cloud of anger on his face.

"Don't lie to me, little one," he growled, then softened as she pulled away in fear. "I'm sorry Lana, I should have taken better care of you. It's my fault you got hurt, not yours. I shouldn't have snapped at you like that."

"Don't be ridiculous, Micah," she put her good hand over his." You've done nothing but look after me since you found me yesterday. Hell, you were even making me coffee when I fell. It's my own stupid fault. I'm always doing dumb stuff like that." He shook his head, remorsefully.

"You know, if you were mine, you would have earned yourself two punishments already today, and it's not even breakfast yet."

"I - I would?!" She stared at him, wide-eyed.

"Yes, ma'am. One for getting out of bed when you're supposed to be resting and two for talking badly about yourself. No little girl of mine would be allowed to call herself dumb or stupid."

"You would really punish me for that?"

"You bet your little bottom I would! I'd make it a bad one, too. Stand in the corner with a bar of soap in your mouth, and that's just for starters." She swallowed hard and looked down, suddenly feeling abashed. The last thing she would ever want to do is disappoint him. That in and of itself was very telling, she realized.

"Please don't be mad at me," she said quietly.

"Oh darlin'," he said softly. "Daddies don't punish because they're mad. They punish because they want to look out for you and keep you safe."

"Really? I've never had a Daddy before." The confession slipped out before she even realized what she was saying. She hadn't really intended on telling him that but there it was.

"You haven't?!" It was his turn to be shocked. "But you're so perfect!" She blushed, and he looked away, scratching his head nervously. She wasn't used to being complimented so blatantly, but she liked how warm it made her feel inside.

"I've had boyfriends. I've just never told any of them about, you know ..." She trailed off, still a little embarrassed about what she was even though she knew it was silly. After all, he was the same way.

"About being a little?" he finished for her. He nodded sympathetically. "It can be scary, I know. I've had more than one woman head for the hills after I told them that I'm a Daddy. But I still feel like honesty is the best policy. Better to be honest and upfront about what you want than end up unhappy and with the wrong person. Which is why you would actually have three punishments because you lied about your wrist being ok just a few minutes ago." She pulled Bernard closer to her instinctively as if he could protect her from these hypothetical punishments.

"You wouldn't even go easy on me for lying to make you feel better?" He shook his head firmly.

"Absolutely not. If you're hurt, you'd better tell your Daddy right away. Your comfort and safety are more important than anyone's ego. In fact, if he doesn't do everything in his power to make it right, then he ain't worth the name Daddy, you understand me, little girl?" She nodded at him, wide-eyed, and bit her lip. The forceful tone in his voice made her whole body go hot, and she suddenly felt lost in his sea-green eyes.

"Let me hear you say it," he said, giving her a hard look that said that he meant business.

"I understand, Micah," she said in a soft, shaky voice.

"Good," he said sighing. "There are a lot of predatory creeps out there who like to call themselves Daddies and I'd hate to see you get mixed up with one of them. But never mind all that, we'd better get you dressed so we can get you to the hospital."

"Will you -" she hesitated and blushed.

"What is it, baby girl? You can ask me." She could feel herself getting wet when he called her baby girl, and she stammered for a moment before she could regather her thoughts.

"Will you help me out of my diaper? I don't want the people at the hospital to see."

"Of course, I will! You'll have to go commando, though. I didn't think to grab your bag from the car. Sorry, I didn't know about the mudslide yet, I was just thinking about getting you to the hospital."

"That's ok. It's only for a few hours." She lay back so that he could loosen her diaper and scoot it off of her. Maybe it was her imagination, but she thought she saw him sneak a little peek this time around. So maybe she wasn't the only one feeling the chemistry. She had a wild urge to spread her legs for him and show off, something that was very out of character for her. Now was definitely not the time for that, anyway. Quickly, he slid her pants on and helped her get them over her hips.

Once they were on, he seemed a bit more relaxed. He helped her sit back up and went to get a comb for her hair. Delicately, he ran it through her gnarled knots until it was shiny and smooth. Lana was at a loss for words. She had never felt so pampered before. She loved the gentle way he ran his fingers through her hair and how close he was to her on the bed. She could feel his warmth radiating from him, and she wanted to lean into it and be wrapped up in his arms again.

"I'm sorry that I don't have a spare toothbrush or anything," he said, breaking the comfortable silence.

"That's ok," she said dreamily. She was so enraptured by his brushing that her mind felt a million miles away. He stopped combing her hair and touched her forehead, concerned.

"Are you ok? Is the dizziness coming back?" She snapped herself out of her reverie.

"Oh no, I'm fine, I was just spacing out a little." He squinted at her skeptically. "Are you sure? You aren't fibbing again?"

"No, I promise. No fibbing." She made a little X over her chest with her finger, crossing her heart. He laughed and nodded, throwing his hands up in mock surrender.

"Ok, ok, I believe you." He looked at her and seemed almost sad for a moment. "Well, the roads should be just about cleared up. We need to get you checked out by the doctor, and I don't want to wait for another minute. Sit tight while I get the truck warmed up."

He got up from the bed but lingered by the doorway. "Stay put, little one," he said firmly.

"I promise," she said sweetly, noticing the way his cheeks turned a little pink at the lilting tone in her voice.

Quit flirting. She chastised herself. *He doesn't want a dumb baby like you.* Then she realized that he might, actually. Except he wouldn't like it if she called herself dumb, he had said so himself. Lana flushed at the possibility of having a real-life Daddy of her very own before she put the thought out of her head.

Even if he were interested, which wasn't a guarantee, she was only here for the summer. And she'd just had her heartbroken. Nothing about this was practical or sensible. She could practically hear Barb now, telling her that a fun summer fling was just the thing to get over a broken heart, but that just wasn't Lana's style. She was the type who only had sex when she was in a committed relationship, one that had the potential to last beyond a few weeks.

On the other hand, maybe it's time for a change in style, she thought as Micah came back and bent down to take her into his strong, burly arms. Again, he scooped her up as if she weighed nothing. It was thrilling to be carried like that. He carried her with such ease that she felt like she was flying as he carried her to his truck.

He sat her down on the front seat and buckled her in. They drove in silence as Micah navigated the narrow mountain path. The road Lana had come in was a fairly wide dirt road but what Micah's hunting lodge was on could charitably be called a path. They turned a sharp corner and the trees cleared. Suddenly Lana could see how high up the mountain they were. It had been so dark when she came in last night that she didn't get to fully appreciate the landscape. She gasped as she saw a deep valley below them, blanketed in pine trees.

"How high up are we?" she asked, her nose pressed up against the window.

"Not that high, actually. The mountains in Georgia are at a low altitude compared to other mountain ranges because they're older."

"They're still higher up than anything you'll find in Florida." She clenched her eyes shut as they went around another steep curve in the road and suddenly questioned if the breathtaking view was really worth it. At least she didn't have to drive. She would be in tears, trying to navigate these narrow turns. They hit a hole in the road, and she squeaked loudly. He put his hand out and put it on her knee, and instantly her fear melted away.

"Are you ok, little one?" Every time he called her that, her body felt warm and glowy all over. She cleared her throat and nodded.

"Yes, I was just startled." His hand lingered on her knee, and she found herself hoping that he would leave it there. He hit a slippery patch on the road, however, and needed both hands on the wheel. She noted with a thrill that he gave her leg a little squeeze before removing his hand. They encountered a few downed limbs along the way, one of which was so big that Micah had to get out of the truck to move it, but for the most part, the roads were a lot more drivable than they had been the night before. Soon, they connected with the paved road which then connected to the main road into town.

As they pulled into the hospital parking lot, Lana swallowed hard, dreading what was coming next. This was probably the last she would see of Micah, which made her sadder than she was prepared for. She had no idea how to initiate a summer love affair, but she was pretty sure a hospital parking lot was not the best place for it.

"Well, thanks for rescuing me. I don't know

how I can ever repay you." Reluctantly, she put her hand on the handle to get out.

"You're welcome but don't think for one second that I'm going to let you hobble into the hospital by yourself. Stay put." He came around and lifted her out of the truck, carrying her all the way inside. Again, he had struck her speechless. She really didn't know what to say in response to such kindness. To her surprise, he stayed with her, even after they got her a wheelchair. He stayed while she waited for a room and while the doctor took a look at her. He stayed in the room when they wheeled her off for x-rays and was even still there waiting for her when they got back.

The doctor came into the room after a long wait to say that nothing was broken but that she would need to stay off her feet for a few days. With plenty of rest and ice, it would heal fairly quickly. As she wrote Lana some prescriptions, Micah announced that he would pull the truck around. When they wheeled her out, he lifted her out of the wheelchair and back in his truck.

"Where is the cabin you rented? We need to get you tucked back into bed right away." She blushed, a little flustered at how much attention he was showing her. Mike probably would have just dropped her off and then called her a cab if this had happened while they were still together. Lana gave him the address and tried to come up with the words to express her gratitude. She snuck little peeks at him while they drove, flushing every time she looked at his handsome face and found herself wondering what it would feel like to be pinned down under his massive frame. She had always had thoughts like that but had never had the courage to ask for it. Something told her that with him, she wouldn't have to ask and that just made the thought all the more thrilling. She got so lost in that thought that before she knew it, they were pulling into the rental office.

"Sit tight. I'll grab the key from the dropbox," he said. As he walked away from the truck, Lana couldn't stop watching his firm backside and muscled thighs. On his way back, she noted how nice the front view was as well. His jeans were hugging his package tightly. He handed her the keys as he got back in, brushing her fingers with his. Just that slight contact was enough to make her feel an ache between her legs.

"I'll drop you off, I'm sure you're beat, and then go back into town to get your prescriptions filled."

"Thank you, Micah. Really, I don't know what to say. You've been so kind to me." He reddened and seemed at a loss for words himself, scratching his head in that embarrassed way that he had.

"Oh, I couldn't just leave you stranded," he said, seeming to shrug it off. He didn't seem to realize that most people might have done exactly that. The fact that he didn't know what a special soul he was just made him even more endearing to her. He would never lord it over her or ask for special favors in return for being a decent human being. It was a refreshing change of pace for Lana. He found her cabin easily, just a couple of miles from the main office. It was a tiny little thing, advertised online as a lover's nest, a prefab affair made of pressed fiberwood made to look like a log cabin. He unlocked the door and turned on all the lights before coming back to carry her inside. He took her straight to the bedroom and gently lowered her onto the bed. For several minutes, he fussed around with pillows and blankets, making sure that she was comfortable. He brought in a glass of water and set it down on the bedside table.

"I'll be back in a couple of hours, do you need me to carry you to the bathroom before I go?" She shook her head. One of the many tests at the hospital had been a urinalysis, and she didn't have to go again just yet. He brushed her hair back and nodded. His hand on her forehead felt so nice that her eyes fluttered closed and she smiled before she could catch herself. She was exhausted and just wanted to curl up in his arms and sleep the rest of the day away.

"Ok," he said softly, his voice sounding suddenly thick with emotion or possibly just lust.

Maybe it was just her hopeful imagination. "I'll go by your car and get your bags out so you'll have everything that you need. I can call a tow truck when I get back and have it taken to a shop. With any luck, they'll have it repaired by the time you're back on your feet."

"You're so good to me," she said drowsily, already half asleep. He tucked her in and went to leave but hesitated for a moment. He bent down and kissed her forehead softly before leaving quietly. Lana fell asleep with a very big smile on her face.

Chapter 5

Micah tried to will his erection away as he drove into town, but thoughts of sweet little Lana plagued him all the way back to town. The fact that she was sick and injured did little to stop him from imagining her pretty pink lips wrapped around his cock which just made him feel all the more guilty for having those thoughts.

She doesn't need you creeping on her right now, he told himself. He couldn't help but kiss her on her forehead when he put her to bed. She looked so sweet and angelic lying there. The kiss had put a smile on her face, and that left him with the hope that there could be something between them someday, but right now she needed to rest and heal. He turned on the radio and hoped that would be enough to distract him. Unfortunately, every song seemed to be a love song, and that only reminded him of her.

He finished his errands as quickly as he could, eager to get back to check on Lana. She had already proven herself to be stubborn and hard-headed in the short time he had known her. He wasn't prepared for the way his heart had dropped when he came in and saw her crumpled on the floor, clutching her arm in pain, and he hoped like hell that he wouldn't return to find her like that again.

Despite his impatience to get back to Lana, he decided that he had better stop for groceries and supplies on the way back to the cabin. Once he was back, he didn't intend on leaving her again. Not for a very long time.

***

Lana woke up to the sound of Micah's tires crunching on the pebbled driveway. It seemed to her that he just left, but the dusk outside her window told her many hours had passed. Her bladder was feeling the effects of the passage of time as well. She squirmed under the covers, waiting for Micah to come inside and help her.

She heard him come in through the front door and set down several bags before going back out to the truck to bring in several more. She couldn't be patient anymore. She felt like she was bursting.

"Micah," she called out when she heard him come back inside. "I need you." He came hurrying in, turning on the light. The look on his face was one of worry, and that filled her heart with a warm glow.

"What's wrong, princess?" She gaped at him for a moment. The affectionate nickname seemed to short-circuit her brain.

"I - I - " The words seemed to have gotten stuck in her mouth, and she could only stammer inarticulately. He crossed the room quickly, a concerned look on his face, and frantically felt her forehead.

"I'm ok. I just need help going to the bathroom." Finally, she was able to speak. Micah looked relieved, as though he had been imagining the worst.

"I can do that. Let's get your pants off, little one." She clutched the covers to her chin.

"Can't you just carry me in and let me take care of the rest?" He shook his head.

"Nope, you could fall trying to scoot your pants down. I can't take that chance." She saw the logic in that and reluctantly lowered the sheets. "Don't worry. I promise not to look." He pulled the covers off her and gently began to take off her pants, helping her scoot them over her hips and delicately folding them and putting them on the bed next to her.

"So you don't have to go hopping all around looking for them later," he said. True to his word, he lifted her out of bed without taking a peek. The air was cool on her butt as he carried her, and it felt strangely nice to be exposed that way. Maybe it was because it was usually covered, but the skin on her butt seemed to be extra sensitive.
He slowly and gently lowered her onto the seat

and stood there, waiting. The urgent need to go was suddenly replaced by a consummate shyness as Micah watched her expectantly.

"I can't go if you watch," she said blushing. "Can I have a moment of privacy, please?"

"I'll turn around, but I don't want you to be by yourself if I can help it. I would never forgive myself if you fell and got yourself hurt again."

"I'm not gonna fall," she muttered. He turned around, his face to the wall, but that's as far as he went. She rolled his eyes at his back and decided that if he wanted to stay, then she wasn't going to let that stop her.

It was easier to go once he was no longer looking. She finished up as quickly as she could and flushed the toilet.

"Can I turn around now?" he asked, almost sounding hurt as if she had banished him to the corner like a scolded child. She wondered what he would look like with a pouty lip and tried not to giggle, knowing that would only add insult to injury.

"Yes, you can turn around now," she said, barely managing to keep a straight face. He didn't have pouty lips when he turned around but it was pretty close. Gently, he lifted her back up and carried her back to bed. She reached for her pants but he stopped her with a gentle touch of his hand.

"Wouldn't you rather wear a diaper, little one?" She looked away, still embarrassed that he knew her secret. He gently nudged her chin, pulling her face back toward him. "What's wrong, you're not still feeling embarrassed are you?" For some reason, she suddenly felt on the verge of tears and couldn't answer. She knew it didn't make sense to be ashamed in front of someone who had the same tastes as hers but after a lifetime of hiding it, she was finding it hard to be comfortable with someone knowing. He sat on the bed next to her, looking her deep in the eye.

"Would it help you to know that I find you very sexy in your diaper?" His voice was quiet and husky. She swallowed hard as a wave of heat washed over her entire body. She could only nod as she looked at him wide-eyed. He smiled at her, then picked up her hand and kissed the back of it, keeping her gaze locked onto his green eyes the entire time.

She felt her body flush with heat again, most of all between her legs. No man had ever turned her on so much just by kissing the back of her hand. No man had ever made her feel as intoxicated as he did. Her heart pounded. She hoped that he would kiss her on the lips next, but instead, he got up and came back with a bag of diapers. Again, he averted his eyes as he diapered her. She appreciated him being a gentleman, but at the same time, she wanted to grab his hand and put it between her legs and beg him to ease the ache that had been growing there all day. Or better yet, to hold her down and fuck her into the mattress.

She was so lost in that last thought that he had the diaper in place and was covering her back up with the blanket before she even realized it.

"But I'm not sleepy," she said, looking up at him with big eyes, hoping he would take the hint.

"Doesn't mean you're not staying in bed. Are you hungry? I got you some soup and some mac and cheese. I wasn't sure what all else you like."

"I like chocolate," she said hopefully. It was no toe-curling sex, but it would do for now. He laughed and shook his head.

"Yeah, I figured as much, but that's for dessert. You need something real for dinner." The stern look on his face told her that there was no point in arguing.

"Mac and cheese?" He nodded, deeming that an acceptable choice.

"Coming right up, Princess." He went out to the kitchen and got things going. When he came back, he had a book and a box in his hands. "I saw this adult coloring book and some pencils at the grocery store, so I picked them up. Don't want you going stir crazy up here." He winked as he put them both down on her lap and her stomach did somersaults. She opened the box of pencils. Her face lit up when she saw all the pretty colors. She flipped through the book excitedly, trying to decide which one to color first. Micah watched her for a moment with a smile on his face, enjoying the sight of her enjoying herself, then went back to making dinner. When he returned with a bowl of hot, cheesy noodles, she had already finished half of a mandala.

"Ok, little one, put the coloring away. It's dinner time." She looked disappointed for a moment, but then she smelled the mac and cheese, and her tummy rumbled, reminding her that she had not eaten that day. She reached for the bowl, but Micah put it on the table. "The bowl is hot, be careful."

He picked up the fork and scooped out a bite, carefully blowing on it before bringing it delicately to her mouth. She instinctively opened her mouth and let him feed her. He was already scooping up a second bit before she actually processed what was happening.

"You don't have to feed me, you know," she said, trying to sound more grownup than she felt at that moment.

"I know that, but I'm going to anyway," he said firmly, bringing the fork to her mouth once again. "You need someone to take care of you and not just because you're injured. You just got your heart broke, and you're up here all alone. I want to show you that not all men high tail it and run as soon as things get tough."

She ate in silence for a while, her mind a whirlwind of thoughts. After a few minutes, she finally worked up the courage to ask the question that had been on her mind all day.

"Do you mean … you want to be my Daddy?" He lowered the fork and just looked at her for a moment, his beautiful green eyes had her caught like a deer in the headlights. The question hung in the air and for a moment, Lana's stomach dropped, certain that she had misread something and had offended him greatly. Instead of answering, however, he leaned in and kissed her very softly. His lips were warm and so inviting, she opened up to him without hesitation. He broke off the kiss way too soon for her liking, and she whimpered softly as he pulled away. He ran his thumb over her bottom lip and smiled.

"Yes, baby girl. I would love to be your Daddy." Lana could only stare at him, feeling slightly dazed as though she were in a dream. She knew she should say something, but he had once again rendered her speechless. He was good at doing that, she noted.

"Cool," was the most eloquent thing she could summon to say in response. Inwardly she cringed, feeling like the most awkward person on the planet. He only smiled, seemingly pleased with the response, and continued feeding her. After she finished her dinner, he made her drink an entire glass of water before she could have the chocolate he had gotten her for dessert.

"Aren't you going to get some dinner?" she asked as she happily munched on her treat.

"I will after I've taken care of my princess," he replied. She almost choked on her chocolate. That was easily the most romantic thing anyone had ever said to her. He took the chocolate away after she had only eaten a couple of pieces.

"That's enough for tonight," he said, kissing her on the forehead before she even had a chance to complain. He gave her back her coloring book and pencils. "Finish up your pretty picture while Daddy eats his dinner and cleans up. I'll be back soon."

She colored happily as he went back to the kitchen, her mind full of dreamy sweet thoughts about her new Daddy.

Chapter 6

He came back sometime later. Lana was so wrapped up in her coloring that she wasn't sure exactly how long but she had finished the first mandala and was almost done with a second one.

"It's bedtime, baby girl," he said. "Time to put the coloring away."

"But I'm not tired, Daddy," she said. Her eyes did feel a little on the heavy side, but she was too excited about the recent turn of events to sleep. How could she relax when her stomach was so full of butterflies every time he looked at her?

"Here," he said, handing her a handful of pills. "These will help the pain and help you sleep." She swallowed them all down with a few sips of water. He took the cup from her and put it back on the nightstand. "I can take you to the bathroom before you go to sleep if you want. Or you can use your diaper again tonight if you need to. Don't be shy. Daddy loves changing your diaper for you." Her heart fluttered again. She never thought that she would hear those words, much less than from someone so handsome and kind. How did she get so lucky?

"I'm ok for now. I'll use my diaper if I need to." While Lana didn't usually wet her diaper, she usually just liked wearing it, she did like being changed by Micah. It also had the added benefit of being practical while she was recovering.

Besides, maybe he won't look away now that he is my Daddy. The thought made Lana burn with desire. She imagined herself splayed out before him as he lovingly caressed every inch of her. Her body was flooded by a sudden urgent need.

"Daddy ..." She wasn't sure exactly what to say, how to voice the fiery desire that now gripped her.

"What is it pumpkin?" he asked, sitting on the bed next to her and taking her hand. She wanted him to pin that hand down to the bed, push her legs apart and take her but she knew they shouldn't do that, not yet anyway. It was too soon for her, summer fling or not and she didn't think it would be as much fun while she was injured anyway. But she needed more than that one little kiss from earlier.

"Can I ... can we kiss some more?" She blushed furiously as the words came out. He made her feel so bold and shy at the same time. He grinned at her, and she could feel her heart glowing.

I had better watch myself, she thought. *This one is dangerous.* It would be oh so easy to let herself fall in love with this charming, dominant, Southern gentleman. Especially if he kept flashing her that grin and giving her butterflies just from holding her hand. Even knowing that it was a bad idea that would likely end in heartbreak might not be enough of a deterrent. She would gladly take the heartbreak if it meant giving in to him.

"Just for a minute, little one," he said. "Then you have to get some sleep." He gently caressed her cheek, studying her face. Then, he brought his hand down to under her chin and lifted her face to him. His lips took hers hungrily as he held her face, his tongue bursting into her mouth, tasting her greedily. He kissed her with such fire and passion that it took her breath away and she could only cling to his shirt as he claimed her with his mouth. The heated wetness between her legs only grew worse as she opened herself up to him, surrendering herself to his demanding tongue. When he broke off the kiss, Lana audibly groaned with disappointment. She needed more, a lot more. Micah only laughed and shook his head, however.

"No, little one. It's time for sleep, and if we keep doing that, neither of us will get any sleep at all tonight. Daddy will read you a story if you'd like, that should help you relax. I picked up a romance story and a mystery story, which one would you like?" Lana considered it a moment before deciding that the romance story might make it even harder to sleep than it already would be after that panty-melting kiss. Hearing about the strong hero seducing the vulnerable maiden would only make the heat between her legs grow worse, especially if it was coming from Micah's lips.

"Mystery story, please." Micah nodded and opened the book, clearing his throat before beginning. She lay back and closed her eyes, listening to Micah's soothing velvety voice. She listened until her body quieted, and she was able to sleep.

***

Micah put the book down and quietly tiptoed out of the room. Lana was finally breathing long and even. As he sat down on the couch that would serve as his bed that evening, he felt his cock throb uncomfortably in his pants. It had not gone down since that deep sexy kiss from his baby girl, even after reading to her for almost half an hour. Watching her sweet face as she drifted off to sleep had done nothing to remedy the situation either. He shifted himself on the couch, trying to find a comfortable position so that he could relax and get some sleep.

He had not planned on things progressing so quickly. He had wanted to wait until she was better healed. She would need to be in good health to endure the things he was planning on doing to her. All he had been able to think about was all the different ways that she could pleasure him and all the different ways that he could make her cum. It was going to be all the harder to resist her if she was going to be asking him for kisses like that. He cursed under his breath and took his throbbing cock out, spitting into his hand. He was going to have to relieve this tension if he was going to keep his hands to himself.

All he could think about was having Lana's sweet lips wrapped around his cock, moaning softly as she licked and nuzzled his shaft. He had accidentally caught a peek of her little pink pussy earlier, and it had driven him wild ever since. Now he imagined her completely naked, on her knees before him. He ached to fondle her perfect perky breasts as she pleasured him slowly and sensually, licking every inch of him with her sexy pink tongue.

A ragged sigh escaped his lips as he stroked himself slowly, enjoying the mental image. The fact that she had never had a Daddy before was strangely intriguing to him, and he looked forward to showing her all of the fun that could be had. He wanted to show her how to live the lifestyle safely and healthily but, more selfishly, he also wanted to train her on how to be a good little for her Daddy. He tried not to think of it as training her for himself. She would be back in Florida by the end of the summer. That thought was just a little too much reality at the moment. Better think about how much fun they could have for now, how cute she would look begging him for his cum and how even cuter she would look with it sprayed all over her pretty face. The thought was too much for his lust addled brain, and he was cumming just as soon as he pictured it.

My princess, he thought as he erupted,

coating his hand, shirt, and pants with his hot, sticky jizz. He sat there, breathless and gripping his still-hard cock, dreams of Lana still running through his head. It had barely been enough to take the edge off, but it would have to do for now. He cleaned himself off quickly and collapsed onto the couch, hoping to rest.

Chapter 7

Lana slept most of the time over the next few days, and Micah was beginning to go a little stir-crazy with no one to talk to. He risked going back to his cabin to get a few books and other things to keep him entertained but only after making Lana pinky promise not to move from the bed before he got back. She promised him and swore to be a good girl, and he believed her, already trusting her implicitly even though they had known each other for a very short time.

On the way back, however, he regretted that. She was so sleepy from the pain medicine that he was scared that she would roll out of bed by accident. He kicked himself for being selfish and leaving her there all alone, certain that he would return to find her crumpled on the floor once more. Of course, all the worrying was for nothing. She was still tucked safely away in bed when he got back to the cabin. As he sighed in relief and rushed to her side, he silently swore to himself that he wouldn't leave the cabin again until she was completely healed.

Within a few days, Lana was feeling better enough to complain about being bored. He let her sit on the couch and watch TV but still insisted on carrying her around wherever she needed to go and waiting on her hand and foot.

"My ankle doesn't even hurt that much anymore," she had complained when he still wouldn't even let her go to the bathroom by herself.

"Not good enough," he had said. "Talk to me when it doesn't hurt at all anymore. Until then, you're not walking anywhere." She knew she should have hesitated at that, telling him that she was a grown woman who could damn well take care of herself, but the truth was that she melted inside over how special it made her feel to be babied to this degree. It was easy to tell that his overprotective behavior came from a place of genuine concern. He was constantly checking on her comfort levels and asking her if there was anything she needed. She had never felt like the center of anyone's world before, and it was a feeling that she hoped she would have to get used to.

Bath time was awkward. He had offered to bathe her, but she felt like that was perhaps too intimate too fast, at least for her. And she'd only hurt her wrist and ankle, after all. It wasn't strictly speaking necessary. As pleasant as it sounded to be bathed by him, she wanted the first time he saw her completely naked to be under somewhat more romantic circumstances. The compromise was that Micah would place Lana in the empty tub fully dressed and she would undress and fill the tub. It was admittedly a little weird, but it would work, for now, they decided.

They snuggled on the couch, spending their days in quiet companionship. Micah read and Lana colored most of the time, or they would watch a movie together. They kissed every so often, but Micah always stopped her when she tried to take it further.

"Don't you want to?" she had asked, frustrated by how slow he wanted to take things. She was usually the one who wanted to slow things down, not the other way around. It was a bit bruising to the ego. He had taken her face in his hands and looked deeply into her eyes before responding.

"Baby girl, of course, I do. The problem is, once I start, I'm not going to stop. Daddy is going to fuck you over and over until I'm satisfied. I'm going to make you come so hard and so often that you're not going to be able to remember your own name. So get your rest now, little one. You're going to need it." He had run his thumb lightly over her bottom lip and then kissed her softly. Lana felt like her whole body was on fire, just from a few simple words. No one had ever spoken to her that way before. Sex had always been a quick activity before bed. Micah made it sound like an all-day event. She wanted so badly for him to push her down onto the couch and take her then and there but he only calmly went back to his book as though he were in no hurry whatsoever.

Finally, the day came for her follow up appointment with the doctor. Micah drove her into town, stopping for some ice cream on the way to sooth Lana's nerves. She didn't have a full-on phobia of hospitals or anything, but she had confessed to him a few days before that doctors made her a little bit nervous. The fact that he remembered and wanted to help her feel better absolutely melted her heart. The doctor gave her a clean bill of health and told her that she could walk on her ankle again and do light activities. She would still take it easy for a while, however, nothing too strenuous.

"Can she have sex?" Micah interjected. He had been sitting quietly in the corner of the room up until that point. The doctor looked a little confused but replied that she didn't see any reason why not. Micah only nodded and didn't have anything else to say for the rest of the appointment. He let her walk on her own pack to the truck but insisted that she take a hold of his arm, just in case. Lana's foot felt one hundred percent better, but she was happy to be able to hold on to his arm for other reasons.

They drove back in silence. Lana wasn't sure what Micah was thinking about but she certainly only had one thing on her mind. The wait was finally over. The doctor had said so herself, and she could finally get what she had been craving for the past several days. Micah, and a lot of him.

She snuck a peek at him, but he seemed as calm as ever. Feeling bold, she reached over and put her hand on his leg. He kept both eyes on the road but took one hand off the wheel to hold hers, squeezing it firmly. He didn't let go for the rest of the drive.

Chapter 8

They had barely taken two steps into the cabin when Micah grabbed her by the arm and pulled her close to him. He wrapped her in his huge arms and looked down at her, drinking in every detail of her face before kissing her deeply. His hungry tongue pushed into her mouth and tasted her like he was starving for her, his arms gripping her so tightly that she could barely breathe. She opened up to him, moaning into his mouth as he explored her with his tongue. His hands began to explore her body as well, running over the curves of her hips and butt. He started to reach under her top but stopped, pulling back from the kiss.

"Get in that bedroom right now, little girl," he growled. Lana's knees instantly grew weak in response to his sexy dominance, but she did as she was told, scurrying off to the bedroom as quickly as she could with Micah right behind her.

"On the bed," she heard him command from behind her as he closed the bedroom door. She kneeled on the bed and waited for him. It was almost dusk now and she just barely could see him, waiting by the door in the shadow.

"Take off your shirt," he said, his voice so low and demanding it sent shivers through her. This was so completely new to her, being told what to do in bed, that she hesitated for a moment. "Baby girl, I expect you to do what I say when I say it. Is that understood?" She nodded, the words filling her with a needy heat and making it hard to think. He seemed to radiate lust and dominance, and it made her feel almost intoxicated by him. This was what she had been longing for her entire life, and it was finally happening.

"Let me hear you repeat it. I want to make sure you truly understand what I'm telling you." His voice was almost a whisper now, but every fiber of her being was attuned to him, waiting for what he would tell her to do next, eager to obey him. It was like a compulsion within her.

"I will do what you say when you say it." Her voice sounded dreamy and distant; the demanding need between her legs only growing stronger. As she said the words, she felt the weight and the significance of what she was promising, and it excited her. She couldn't wait to be his, really and truly his.

"Good," he purred. "Now take off your shirt like a good girl." She pulled the t-shirt over her head and tossed it to the floor. He didn't say anything for a moment, just drank in her naked body in with his eyes.

"You're so beautiful, baby girl," he said, making her blush deeply. No one had ever looked at her so intensely before, and it was making her feel self-conscious. Hearing his reassuring words made her glow with pride even through her bashfulness. She had never tried to be provocative before so she moved on instinct, running her hands slowly over her stomach and hips for his visual pleasure. Judging from the sharp inhale from Micah, it worked.

"Take off your pants," he growled. The whisper was gone, his voice now thick and velvety, and she imagined him as the big bad wolf, lurking in the shadows. Slowly, she unbuttoned her jeans, unpeeling them down her hips. Even though she couldn't see his eyes, she could feel him track her every move. Knowing that he was watching her, aroused by her was such an aphrodisiac. She lay back on the bed and kicked her pants off and lounged back on the pillows, savoring the feeling of anticipation that sent tingles all over her.

"Open your legs," came the next command. "I want to see what is mine." Slowly, she parted her knees, thoroughly intoxicated by his domination over her. Her pussy was dripping wet already even though he had barely touched her. She was fairly certain that she would be able to see how aroused she was from the dark spot left by her juices. He made a noise somewhere between a moan and a growl and rubbed his cock through his jeans but made no move to take them off or come towards her.

"You're mine now, baby girl." His voice was hypnotic, thick with lust. "Every part of you, every inch of you now belongs to me. Do you understand me?"

"Yes, Daddy." Lana felt breathless. Her body yearned for him more powerfully than she ever thought was possible.

"I want to hear you repeat it, little girl. What are you?"

"I'm yours. I belong to you, every inch of me."

"That's right, little one. Now let Daddy see those perfect tits." Lana gasped as her core clenched with desire and she hurriedly obeyed, eager to give him whatever he asked for. As she tossed the bra aside and proudly displayed herself for him, she heard him growl "good girl," and she was filled with glowing pride. His praise erased all self-doubt. At last, he came towards her, his slow sensual movements heavy with the promise of things to come. He had a raw hunger on his face that made her tremble inside, made her need to be consumed by him. He joined her on the bed, kneeling in between her legs, and gazed down at her. With a contented sigh, he ran his hands over her breasts. Her nipples hardened and came alive under his touch, and his grasp became firmer, more demanding. He bent down, claiming her mouth briefly with his own before working his way downward, devouring her neck and breasts. He teased her with his lips and tongue, nibbling lightly at her flesh. His hands continued to explore her body as well, pulling her hips against him so that she could feel the bulge of his cock against the thin material of her panties. Lana threw her head back against the pillows, moaning with delight as he lavished her body with attention. As he slid his hands over the outside of her panties, she was overwhelmed by the pleasure that washed over. The way he gripped her lightly, feeling her wetness against the palm of his hand, felt so deliciously possessive. She ground her pelvis against his hand, her body seeking more to satisfy its urgent craving. He chuckled with his mouth around her nipple.

"Are you already that needy, baby?" he asked, his voice teasing and playful. "Daddy has just barely gotten started with you, little one." As he spoke, he hooked his fingers into her panties and peeled them down until they were past her feet, tossing them aside. He grinned like a satisfied cat as he looked at her, now completely naked. She felt exposed and vulnerable in a way that made her body flush with desire. If she wasn't able to relieve some of this pressure soon, she felt like she might lose her mind. It had been building between them for so long that it was now an all-consuming need. He lowered himself on the bed, putting his face so close to her pussy that she could feel his breath against her. He stared at her adoringly and traced a finger lightly around her labia, the gentle touch making her thighs quiver. Slowly, he explored her with his finger, tracing over her folds and dipping into the wetness pooled in between, staring at her intently the entire time as if he were memorizing her. She squirmed and moaned as he teased her, the soft sensations not nearly enough to quell her craving.

"Tell Daddy what you need, little one," he purred, grinning up at her, clearly enjoying the sight of her writhing and moaning. Her body cried out for relief, but the thought of putting it into words made her burn with embarrassment. His finger hovered near her entrance, waiting.

"Please, Daddy," she gasped and yearned her hips forward, desperate to be filled by him, to ease the ache within at last.

"Not until you tell Daddy what you need. You can ask me for anything, baby girl. Just say it." Lana found that she was beyond caring. She had no time for modesty anymore. Her body was on fire, and only one thing could sate her.

"Please make me cum, Daddy. I need you so badly, please!"

"Good girl," he purred as he slipped his finger inside of her at last, never taking his eyes off her as she threw her head back and moaned in sweet relief. Still looking up at her, he put his warm, soft tongue against her aching clit, moaning against her as she gyrated her hips. He pumped his finger in and out of her, hitting her most sensitive spot with every thrust into her hungry pussy. She watched him as she slid her clit up and down his tongue, working herself towards an orgasm. She had never seen a man so happy just to give her pleasure before, and she couldn't take her eyes away. She clutched the sheets of the bed. Her thighs clenched as she worked herself against his tongue, frantically meeting the thrust of his finger deep inside of her. All at once, she came on his tongue, ecstasy moving like an unstoppable force from the center of her being and rippling all over her. She clutched the back of his head, pulling him closer as she climaxed, and he pumped his finger into her harder. When she finally relaxed back against the mattress, breathless and panting, he gave a deep, satisfied sigh.

"You taste so good, baby girl." He nuzzled her clit again, making her jump slightly. "I could stay down here for hours and hours." Gently, he kissed the spot just above her clit, making her twitch slightly, then got up to his knees. He stripped his shirt off, revealing a broad, hairy chest, thick arm muscles, and toned abs. Everything about him was so attractive to her, just looking at him drove her wild. He looked so delicious that she had to sit up and run her hands over his chest and abs, appreciating his masculine form.

"Daddy, you're so sexy," she whispered and slowly began to kiss his stomach, her hands reach for the clasp on his jeans, ready to claim her prize.

"Thank you, little one," he said and sighed in pleasure as she unzipped his pants, her tender lips inching toward the elastic band of his underwear. His hands ran gently over her hair as she began tugging on his jeans and underwear, unable to get them over his hard, muscular thighs. "Need some help?" He lay back on the bed, effortlessly kicking off his pants and spread out on the bed, displaying his nude form for her to enjoy.

He looked completely comfortable being nude, even seemed to enjoy having her eyes on him. She thought that on any other man, that kind of confidence would have come across as arrogant but on Micah, it was incredibly alluring. His cock was enormous and already throbbing, and she longed to have it inside of her, to show him the same pleasure that he had shown her. Gazing at it with a slightly dazed hunger, she stroked it lightly with her hand, enjoying how his face went slack with pleasure at her touch.

"Daddy's turn," she purred and bent down to kiss the tip lightly. She closed her eyes as she tongued the underside of the tip, savoring the taste of him. He put his hand under chin, lifting her face slightly.

"Look at me," he said. She opened her eyes again to see him staring down at her with an intensity she had never seen before. Her face got hot with embarrassment, and she suddenly felt very self-conscious. "Keep going, little one. Daddy wants to watch you suck his cock, don't be shy."

She smiled, his naughty words filling her with encouragement, and took the tip of him into her mouth. His breath quickened, and he stroked her cheek, gazing down at her with open adoration. Keeping her eyes locked on his, she began to work his shaft further and further down her throat, getting a thrill from the look of agonized pleasure on his face. That look emboldened her, made her begin to pick up her pace with enthusiasm, loving the effect she was clearly having on him.

"Stop, baby girl," he suddenly growled, pulling her up. She almost whined with disappointment, but he pulled her up for a deep kiss, his erection pressing between them as he held her close. She melted against him as his greedy tongue pushed into her mouth, his teeth lightly grazing her lip. "You almost made me cum, little one. I'm not done with you yet." He grabbed a handful of her hair and tugged her head to the side, exposing her neck. He held her like that as he kissed and bit her neck, making her squirm with desire. Despite the powerful orgasm she'd had just minutes before, her body was already on fire, yearning for more. She gripped his broad shoulders as he devoured her neck, moaning softly as the mild pain in her scalp only intensified her need. She felt helpless pinned against him like that, and that helplessness was exhilarating.

With his free hand, he grabbed the flesh of her buttocks, digging his fingers into the skin as he pulled her closer against his throbbing member. With a vicious growl, he brought his hand down sharply onto her ass, spanking her forcefully. Lana was not prepared for the pain or the way it made her body clench with the desire. She moaned loudly as he brought his hand down, again and again, keeping her pinned against him with his fist in her hair. The flesh of her buttocks stung more and more with every blow, and she could feel her pussy responding with an aching need. She spread her legs, straddling him, and started squirming against him as he spanked her. Her body sought out what it needed, inching him closer and closer to her entrance, desperate to have him inside of her. He growled in her ear, bringing his hand even harder down onto her buttocks.

"What is it that you're after down there, little one? Hmm?" She knew he wanted her to voice her need once again, but it was impossible to think when he was spanking her so firmly, much less speak. She whined and writhed against him, but he only spanked her again, his blows beginning to come harder and harder. Part of her wanted to stay like that forever, locked in perpetual anticipation as he masterfully teased her, inflaming her desire.

"Tell Daddy what you want," he said, his tone indicating that he was losing patience. She opened her legs wider as the tip of his cock brushed her labia. He was so close to being inside her. It would take just a tiny little thrust. But he had her locked in place with his strong arms. She could not wiggle her way onto his cock. He would not give her what she so desperately needed until she asked for it, but his methodical spanking filled her head with a fog of pain and pleasure, too adrift in a sea of bliss to move. *The sweetest torture*, she thought distantly, feeling as though she had entirely lost control of her body. Suddenly, he shifted her weight, flipping her onto her back and kneeling between her knees. She gasped loudly as he began to run the tip of his cock over her clit, rubbing it in slow circles over her swollen nub.

"Do you want Daddy's cock, little one?" he said with a husky voice. She stared down, fascinated by the sight of his cock gliding over her, and nodded. "Say it." She no longer felt frozen, the sensation of his rigid member against her aching sex demolished all of her inhibitions and the words came tumbling out at last.

"I want your cock, Daddy. Please, I need it, please fuck me!" With a satisfied sneer, he plunged into her, roaring with satisfaction as he buried himself inside of her to the hilt. Lana made a roar of her own, grasping his buttocks to pull him closer. Her entire body felt alive as he stretched her open, taking her hard and fast. He unleashed his passion onto her, rutting into her like a crazed animal. His hands twisted into her hair, yanking her hair back as he drove himself into her furiously.

"Is that what you wanted, kitten?" he growled into her ear.

"Yes, fuck me hard!" Lana had never experienced such heat, such passion, and she wanted it to go on and on. As his thick cock split her open again and again, she could feel another climax building. She raked her nails over his back and buttocks, wild with pleasure.

"Good girl," he laughed playfully. "Let it all out, princess." He reached down and began to stroke her clit with his thumb as he pounded into her, overwhelming her with ecstasy. The double stimulation was too much for her, and another orgasm broke over her, stronger than the first, as she thrashed her head from side to side. She let herself go completely, trembling and moaning beneath him.

"Oh fuck, baby girl, you're so tight around my cock." As Lana's quaking orgasm began to recede, Micah's thrusts quickened. She could feel his manhood grow even harder inside of her, throbbing on the edge of release. "Look at me." Shyly, she peeked up at him. He yanked her hair harder to bring her face closer to his, holding her face firmly with his other hand. The possessive way his fingers dug into her face gave her a sense of belonging that she never thought possible before that moment.

"You're mine," he said, holding her gaze with his sea-green eyes. "Say it." She felt her heart melt open in a way it never had before, leaving her feeling raw and vulnerable. Every cell in her body knew it was true, knew that this man was her future.

"I'm yours, Micah," she whispered. He pulled her face to his for a kiss, deep but tender.

"All mine," he whispered, his breath hot against her lips. His rhythm suddenly faltered, and she could feel his grip on her hair tightened as his body went rigid. His cock throbbed and twitched inside of her as he filled her up with his seed. With one final shudder, he collapsed against her and buried his face in her neck, his breath ragged. They clung to each other, Lana surprised at how comfortable she was with Micah's weight on top of her. His arms gripped her tightly, holding her close against her body as he lay with his still-hard cock inside of her, seemingly in no hurry to move. She had never felt so safe, so contented. She held him close and kissed his sweaty forehead, brushing his hair aside as he caught his breath, and thought about how she would love to stay like that forever.

Chapter 9

When Lana woke again, it was pitch black dark outside. Micah was sprawled out on the bed beside her, naked and snoring softly. She felt a wave of affection suddenly, coupled with a desire that had only been partially quenched by their lovemaking earlier. As quietly as she could, she lowered herself until her face was level to his member. Even soft, it was impressive to look at, laying across his toned belly like a python lying in wait. Gingerly, she took the head into her mouth, barely applying pressure as she ran her tongue over the sensitive tip. He made a soft noise but didn't open his eyes. As she took him further into her mouth, she could feel his cock begin to twitch as the blood flooded in. He still tasted of their shared juices, and she moaned lightly as she tasted him. As he grew harder, she began to apply more pressure, delighting in how responsive he was. With a happy sigh, he finally opened his eyes. Looking down at her with sleepy affection, he smiled and ran his fingers lightly through her hair.

"Are you already greedy for more, little one?" he purred. "Mmm, I love seeing you so needy for my cock." Grabbing a handful of her hair, he pushed her down further onto him, his partially erect member sliding easily down her throat. It was delightful, feeling a fullness in her throat without feeling like she had to gag, and she swallowed him greedily. As he grew fully erect, she struggled to keep him down her throat, choking slightly around his thick member. He stroked her face as she pleasured him, testing her own limits as she took him deeper and deeper.

"Oh fuck, kitten!" Micah threw his head back against the pillow. "That's so good. You're doing so good. Yeah, choke on it, baby." Lana felt almost hypnotized, her body tingled with desire as she gagged and choked on him. Never before had she gotten such satisfaction from giving a blowjob, had never felt this desire to consume someone entirely like she did with Micah. His obvious enjoyment egged her on, made her want more and more of him.

"Princess, you're going to make me cum," he groaned, gripping her hair harder. "Do you want Daddy to cum in your mouth?" Lana nodded and began sucking him off faster, stroking his balls lightly with her finger tips. She stared at his handsome face, enjoying the look of ecstasy on his chiseled face as he grunted and filled her mouth with his cum. She swallowed it all eagerly, moaning quietly as he held a fistful of her hair, holding her down on his pulsing cock.

"Good girl," he whispered shakily, patting the back of her head gently. With a happy grin, she gently licked up a few droplets of cum that hand landed on his stomach before curling up into his arms. He kissed her, his breath still shaky, and reached down to stroke her aching pussy.

"Oh, sweetie, you're so wet," he purred with a grin. "Why don't you get on up here and sit on

Daddy's face?" Before she could respond, he was grabbing her by her ass and hoisting her up so that she was straddling his shoulders. With a squeal and a giggle, she scooted up so that his tongue met her clit. He gave her pussy a long slow lick, moaning with satisfaction as he tasted her. She grabbed a handful of his silky black hair and ground her hips against him. He grabbed her by the wrists and moved her hands to her bare breasts instead.

"Play with your titties, Pumpkin," he whispered. "Show Daddy how you like to be touched." He went back to twirling his tongue around her clit as she groped herself, pinching her nipples as he studied her closely.

"Harder," he commanded. "I want to see how hard you can take it." She twisted her nipple, the pain combining with the delicious sensations of his tongue lapping at her, and she moaned, grinding herself against his mouth. He grabbed her by the ass, his fingers digging into her flesh as he devoured her.

"Slap your tits," he growled and flicked his tongue lightly across her clit. Tentatively, she smacked her palms on her nipples, intrigued by the sensation. "Harder," he pushed, and she obeyed. She slapped her breasts, again and again, each time a little more forcefully as she found that the pain mixed with pleasure was bringing her close to a climax. He groaned approvingly and smack her ass hard, adding to the intense sensations. She felt her legs grow shaky as she squirmed against his mouth. As he brought his hand down onto her fleshy buttock once more, she could hold back no longer. She twisted her nipples, harder than ever before as wave after wave of intense pleasure washed over her. He grabbed her hips, holding her firmly down on his mouth as she shivered and quaked, her moans echoing off the walls of the small bedroom. As she collapsed back, he caught her, gently easing her down on the mattress. She sighed happily as he wrapped his arms around her again, kissing her deeply. She could taste her own juices on his tongue, and she moaned into his mouth, feeling dirty in the best possible way. She loved the way he stripped her of her inhibitions, making her submit entirely to his desires, opening her up to a whole new world of pleasure.

To her surprise, Micah was already hard again. Eating her out must have aroused him greatly because she could feel him begin to press into her, ready to claim her once again. She opened her legs wider, eager to have him inside of her. She was still sensitive from her climax and shivered with delight as he thrust into her.

"Oh, baby girl, you're so wet," he exclaimed, "Keep taking it just like that. Oh, you're such a good girl." His thick cock claimed her, affirming that she belonged to him. She moaned and grabbed his ass, pulling him deeper inside of her, craving more of him. He seemed to know all the right spots to hit and, even better, made sure to hit them with every stroke.

"Daddy, you feel so good," she cried out, thrashing her head against the pillow as he split her open again and again. With a sigh, he pulled out, grabbing her by the hips and flipping her so that she was up on all fours. Something about the way he manhandled her, putting her exactly where he wanted her, made her feel like his sexy little plaything. As he entered her from behind, she noticed that it was a different sensation. He seemed to fill her up more, going deeper with every thrust. He grabbed her hand, guiding it to touch her clit as he pounded into her.

"Does that feel good, sweetheart?" he asked, grabbing the flesh of her buttocks and pulling them apart.

"Yes, Daddy," she said, rubbing her sensitive spot as his rock hard cock stretched her out.

"Oh princess, your tight little pussy is milking my cock. You're so tight and wet, just for me." She felt him run his thumb over her other entrance and shuddered, totally unprepared for the toe-curling jolt it sent throughout her body. "Do you like that, baby girl?"

"Ooh, Daddy!" she cried out, rocking her hips back to meet his. "Oh, that feels really nice." She had never been stimulated there before and had never thought that she would like it, but as Micah ran circles around her rear entrance, it made her pussy react. He licked his thumb and slowly began to sink it in, moving gradually to allow her body time to adjust to the intrusion. The anal stimulation was sending her close to another orgasm, and she squealed and squirmed with delight, rubbing her clit furiously.

"Oh, kitten, you're so tight. Are you going to come on Daddy's cock again?" She couldn't answer, she could only moan and rub her clit as she clenched around his cock and thumb, orgasming with such force that her legs shook. As her climax subsided, he hammered into her even harder, his thumb digging further into her ass. She started to pull her hand away from her clit, but he slapped her ass hard, making her yelp with pain, and grabbed her wrist, replacing her hand between her legs.

"Did I tell you to stop touching yourself, baby girl?" he growled, smacking her ass again. Lana's eyes rolled back in her head, the thoughts in her head too jumbled from the overwhelming pain and pleasure.

"N-no, Daddy," she managed to stammer out. Obediently, she began running her finger over her sensitive nub once again, trembling with pleasure and he claimed her body with his.

"I told you, once I start fucking you, I'm not going to stop. I'm not going to stop until you can't think or stand. You'll only be able to lay there and take it." She shivered, the image was enticing. Already she felt beyond all words and thought. As she grunted and thrust back against him, she felt like a wild woman, all inhibitions thrown to the wind. It felt so right and natural to give over control to him, to be his puppet made only to please him. The thought made her pussy clench, and she knew that she would soon be orgasming again. He spat on her rear entrance, giving his thumb more slip as he began to work it in and out of her. It was by far the dirtiest thing anyone had ever done to her in the bedroom, and she was shocked to find that she didn't find it disgusting. Rather, his ownership of her allowed her the freedom to be as dirty for him as he wanted her to be.

"Oh, Daddy," she squealed. As both his thumb and his cock slid in and out of her, Lana came so hard that her voice broke and her legs collapsed beneath her. Micah was undeterred, shifting his weight so that he was on top of her and just kept right on fucking her into the mattress just as she had dreamed that he would. She kicked her legs and squealed, the stimulation was too much to handle, and she felt like she was losing her mind.

"So naughty." He groaned and swatted her ass again. "Keep rubbing that clit, little one. If I have to tell you again, I'm going to strap a vibrator to your leg and keep it there all night." Lana obeyed at once, dreading what that much stimulation would do to her already taxed body and mind. She rubbed her clit, helpless against the onslaught of pleasure as Micah continued to use her without mercy. She whined and moaned, her skin growing slick with sweat as she thrashed and kicked underneath him. Just as she was beginning to think that she couldn't take another climax, Micah pulled his thumb out of her ass and replaced it with the tip of his cock. He pulled her hips up and swatted away her hand, touching her clit directly with his large fingers. Slowly, he began to push himself into her, stretching out her rear end with his thick cock. He was slick with her juices and slid in easily yet was careful not to go too quickly lest he hurt her. Lana screamed and thrashed underneath him. It felt more amazing than anything she ever experienced before, so amazing that her tired, over-stimulated body was somehow building to yet another orgasm. He pushed himself past the rim, her tight ass hugging the tip of his cock as he rubbed her clit, driving her mad with pleasure. She thrust her hips back as she got closer, wanting to take more of him inside of her. He let her control the pace, letting her fuck herself with his cock as he rubbed her closer and closer to cumming. She thrust herself all the way back, taking him completely inside her body, and shook with an orgasm so powerful that she couldn't move or make noise, she could only lay there and quake beneath him. It seemed to last forever, her body rigid with ecstasy, but at last, she came down from the peak, utterly exhausted.

"Oh baby girl," he cried out, pulling himself from her With a loud grunt, he let himself go, spraying her back with his cum. It felt so warm as it hit her flesh, so possessive, as though he were marking her as his. The thought sent a contented wave of happiness over her, glowing with pride at being owned by him.

He collapsed his weight onto the bed beside her, lazily wrapping his arm around her waist and pulling her close. She felt like her entire body was made of jello. She felt sore and exhausted but also happier than she had ever felt in her life, and he put his hand on the back of her head and stroked her hair.

"Oh, baby girl. You did so good. Daddy is so proud of you." He held her face up to his for a kiss, his warm lips gentle and soft against hers. She melted into him, savoring the warm feeling of skin on skin. Moving seemed completely out of the question, so they lay in each other's arms for a long time as he stroked her back and hair. Eventually, he disentangled himself from her with a groan, stretching languidly before padding into the kitchen, still naked. He returned with a large glass of water and instructed her to drink all of it.

"You're going to need to stay very hydrated. Daddy has big plans for you over the next few days." The way he said it made her tummy do flips wondering what else he could possibly have in mind. After she finished her water, he tucked her back into bed. It wasn't yet daylight, and they were sure to be able to catch a few more hours of sleep. After he got back into the bed with her, she curled around his large frame once again.

"Get your rest, little one. You're going to need it." He chuckled and kissed her forehead. She smiled and closed her eyes, looking forward to whatever came next.

Chapter 10

True to his word, Micah was hungry for more first thing in the morning. He woke her up by licking her pussy, telling her that they wouldn't be getting up for breakfast until she had five orgasms. At first, she giggled, but by the third orgasm, she was no longer laughing, and by the fifth one she was on the verge of tears. He made her pancakes for breakfast, and they both ate in ravenous silence. As she watched Micah eat, she could feel her body responding to him. It was as though he were training her to associate him with pleasure. Lana smiled and turned her attention back to her plate. If that was the case, she thought, it was working. He suggested that after breakfast, they should go for a hike. The cabin she had rented was attached to a short private trail for the rental company's customers to enjoy.

"Not a long one, of course. We don't want to strain your ankle, after all. But it would be a real shame for you to spend your entire vacation cooped up inside. If you like it and want to try something more challenging or scenic, I know of some other trails around here that I can take you to as well." Lana had never been hiking before, but she was well up for the adventure. She only had a pair of tennis shoes which Micah said would be fine for today. If she eventually wanted to work her way up to a more challenging path, he said that he would buy her new hiking boots.

"You will?" She couldn't help her surprise. It wasn't her birthday, an anniversary, or Christmas.

"Of course, little one. I want to make sure that you have the proper footwear. I always want you to be safe and comfortable. Understood?" She nodded.

"I understand, Daddy," she said and stood on her tiptoes to kiss him.

"What was that for?" It was his turn to be surprised. She only shrugged and smiled at him.

"Just because you're cute." His face reddened a bit, and he scratched his head.

"Let's go, kitten," he said, putting his hand on the small of her back to lead her out of the cabin and into the fresh air. The small gesture was dominant in a nonsexual way that made her go a bit weak in the knees. It was a lovely day, lots of sunshine without being too hot. They stuck to the shade where the late spring air was still fresh and cool. The trail was fairly level and easy to traverse. He checked in with her often, offering to stop to let her rest or even carry her if she needed him too but she declined.

"Really, Micah, I feel fine. Stop worrying."

"Nope, not going to happen," he said and took her hand. "I'm going to keep right on worrying about you, and there is nothing you can do about it little girl." She giggled, glowing from within as he pulled her close to him.

"You are mine now," he whispered in her ear, his hot breath making her pussy clench with need as if he hadn't just spent the entire morning making her scream. He grabbed a handful of her ass, bringing the bulge of his cock against her stomach. She could feel herself getting wet all over again. He looked around surreptitiously to see if anyone was close by. When he saw that there was no one, he looked down at her with an evil grin before pulling her up so that she had to wrap her legs around his waist and carried her off into the trees.

"You are mine," he repeated, pushing her up against the bare trunk of a tree and sliding his hand under her shirt, grabbing a handful of her breasts. He tasted her mouth slowly and sensually, tweaking her nipples as he swallowed her moans. "Are you ready to show Daddy that you truly belong to me?"

"What do you mean?" she asked breathlessly. How else could she show him but what they have already been doing? What more of herself could she give?

"I'm going to use you for my pleasure. I'm going to fuck you and cum in that tight little pussy of yours, but you are not allowed to cum. I want you to still be wet and needy when I'm done with you, waiting desperately for me to use you again. Is that understood?" She gasped, her entire body aching at his words. It was so erotic, the thought of him having such absolute control over her body and mind like that, giving or denying pleasure at his whim. She shivered as the thought about being left wanting more, her craving for him only growing as the day went on.

"Yes, Daddy. I promise not to cum when you use me. I won't cum again until you tell me to."

"Good girl," he growled, putting her back down on her feet. "Now pull your pants down and turn around." Her clit was throbbing as she did what he commanded, her shaking hands pulling at the waistband of her leggings and panties, exposing herself to the daylight. She shuffled her feet, turning her face toward the tree and waited, her skin tingling with anticipation as she awaited his next instructions. He didn't say anything for a long while. She heard the sound of metal on metal as he unzipped his pants, but then there was only silence again. Curiosity made her want to turn to see what he was doing, but her need to obey him kept her facing the tree. He seemed to enjoy making her wait, knowing that the anticipation only made her want him more.

"Bend over," he said at last. She put her hand on the tree to steady herself and bent at the hips, giving him a full view of her pussy and ass. He made a satisfied noise, putting one hand on the silky skin of her bottom, giving her goosebumps as he just barely ran his fingers over her sensitive flesh. He pressed his hard cock against her clit, making her legs tremble slightly. He laughed as he tapped it against, making her jump and twitch with every tap.

"Oh kitten, you're already so wet and needy for Daddy's cock. You just can't get enough of it, can you?" She shook her head and groaned, squirming back against him. He brought his hand down onto her ass hard.

"Can you, kitten?" Instinctively, she knew

what he wanted to hear, and she found herself eager to say it, eager to do anything to please him.

"Please, Daddy. I need you to fuck me again. I need your cock."

"Good girl," he sighed, inching himself into her slowly. Her eyes rolled back in her head as he filled her in an agonizingly slow pace until he was buried in her completely. He held her there for a moment, grabbing her by the hips as he savored the feeling of being so deep inside of her. He began pulling out at that same excruciatingly slow speed. Lana acutely aware of every sensation as he slowly stretched her open, pleasuring her but also leaving her aching for more. Her body cried out for more, and she whimpered, moving her hips to increase the tempo. He only slapped her ass, however, and gripped her hips harder to hold her in place.

"What did I tell you, little girl? You had your fun this morning. Now it's Daddy's turn. Don't move until I'm done with you." Her pussy tightened around him, his words only making her crave him all the more. She whined and gripped the tree as he took his sweet time, seemingly not the least bit concerned that they could be discovered at any moment. She wondered what they would look like to a stranger who happened upon them, what they might think of her. Would they think she was a slut? For some reason, the thought sent a thrill through her.

"I'm sorry. I'll be a good slut for you, Daddy." It seemed to have a similar effect on Micah. He made a strangled noise and slammed his cock into her, suddenly pounding fast and hard, no more teasing. She held on tight, biting her lip to keep from crying out in satisfaction. Every thrust sent a lightning bolt of pleasure through her, and she focused her mind on his cock and the delicious fucking he was giving her.

"Good girl," he whispered. "That's a good little slut." Suddenly, he was pulsing inside of her, grunting as he pumped her full of his seed. With a shaky breath, he began to pull up her panties but didn't pull out just yet. He pumped his partially hard cock into her a few more times, clearly just enjoying the feeling of using her; however, he wished. It felt even more amazing, being fucked with a pussy full of cum, and her body wanted more and more. She felt like she would never get enough of him, no matter how many times they fucked. Finally, he pulled out of her, careful to catch all the semen that dripped out onto her panties. He pulled them up, caked with his cum, and then pulled her pants up as well. He pulled her against him, wrapping one arm around her waist as he kissed her from behind. With the other arm, he gave her pussy a light pat, and she could feel his little present squishing in her underwear. Her face suddenly felt hot, and she knew that she was blushing furiously. This was the kind of thing that Lana had always thought was gross and stupid when Barb would tell her about them. She loved Barb but had always thought that the things she let men do to her were crass and tasteless.

Looks like I owe her an apology, she thought as she squeezed her thighs together, savoring the sensation. He slipped his tongue into her mouth quickly before pulling his pants back up and winking at her.

"That was perfect, baby girl. You're so sexy." He wrapped his arms around her, holding her close. She was still aching for him, but she closed her eyes contentedly, enjoying the hunger. It made her feel so alive and so sexy. He took her by the hand, leading her back to the trail. With every step she took, she had a reminder of who she belonged to. She was sure that there must be a wet spot on her pants and blushed, part of her hoping no one would see while another, dirtier part of her hoped that everyone would. She wanted everyone to know who she belonged to.

Chapter 11

Back at the cabin, Micah said he would make up some lunch and that she should play until it was ready. After all of that physical activity, Lana found that she was starving. She stopped him on the way to the kitchen, however, wanting something else besides food.

"Daddy, will you put me in a diaper please?" She could feel herself going into her little space and wanted to experience that with him. He smiled and kissed her forehead.

"Of course, princess. Daddy will help you out of your sticky panties and into a nice, fresh diaper." She blushed at the reminder that her panties were still full of his cum and even more at how erotic she had found the experience. He was bringing out a whole new side to her, and it was thrilling. He picked her up and carried her to the bedroom, placing her gently on the bed. She lay back and let him take her pants off. He took a moment to admire the stain on her panties from his little present before removing them as well.

"Oh, baby girl, you look so sexy right now," he said as she opened her legs for him. "I can still my cum leaking out of you. You are so perfect." He took a wet wipe and began to delicately clean her off, moving it slowly over her labia as his breath began to quicken.

"Do you ever masturbate in your diaper, sweetheart?" he asked as he pulled one out of the pack.

"No, is that normal?" she asked. He smiled and shook his head.

"There is no normal. Everybody is a little bit different from the next person. I like the way you look in your diaper. I find it very sexy. But not everyone likes them for that reason. Some people just feel comfortable wearing them." She thought about it for a moment as he slid the diaper onto her and fastened it with elastic tabs.

"I think I'm a comfort person. I usually wear them when I'm feeling sad or stressed out, not when I'm feeling horny." He nodded slowly and put her pants back on her.

"Are you feeling sad or stressed out right now?" She considered the question thoughtfully then shook her head.

"No, I just want to be comfortable and be a baby for a while. It's fun and relaxing."

"Well, alrighty then." He kissed her on the forehead again. "Good to know."

"You're not upset that I don't want to do stuff in my diaper?"

"Upset? No, of course not. I still get the pleasure of seeing you happy. What about that could ever make me upset?" She didn't know what to say. He had that effect on her often, she realized, and smiled, kissing him on the cheek.

"Thank you, Daddy. Can I have my pacifier?" He chuckled and fished it out from the nightstand, placing it her mouth, then kissing the handle. Lana giggled, feeling like the luckiest girl in the world.

"Come on, cutie. You can color while I make us lunch." He carried her into the living room and put her down on the floor then brought her her coloring supplies and a couple of stuffies. He watched her play affectionately for a few minutes before going off to prepare their meal.

***

After lunch, Lana took a long nap and awoke to the sounds of Micah cooking dinner. She groggily stumbled into the kitchen to find him frying chicken.

"Hey kitten, you slept the whole day away. Feeling ok?" She nodded and grinned sheepishly. "Yeah. I guess you wore me out today." He laughed and patted the back of her diaper affectionately. "I warned you, little one. I've got an appetite."

"No complaints here." She helped him make dinner and set the table. After they ate, Micah took her hand and kissed it.

"Listen, kitten. My vacation is going to be over soon, and I'm afraid that I'll need to go back to the city."

"The city? Do you mean Atlanta? You don't live out here?"

"No, that's just a hunting cabin, remember?" She scrunched up her face as she recalled something to that effect. "I work as a lawyer in the city. I just come here to get away, but I have to go back to work. Would you want to come with me? There are a lot of fun things we can do in the city together."

"Yeah!" she said excitedly. "And I could stay at your place?"

"Of course, baby girl. Daddy's place is your place, anytime you like. I don't go back to work for a couple of more days, but we could head back to the city early if you'd like and I could show you around." A night of dinner and dancing sounded amazing to Lana. It had been so long since she had been out. Then she remembered that she had mostly only brought hiking clothes, thinking she would be spending most of her time enjoying the outdoors.

"I didn't bring anything dressy, though." She wrinkled her face at the thought of going to a nightclub in yoga pants.

"I guess I'd better take you shopping, then." Her eyes sparkled, and her face lit up.

"Really?!" He laughed and kissed her nose.

"Pumpkin, I would do anything if it meant seeing that look on your face. We'll make shopping our first priority when we get to town tomorrow." She truly felt like a princess all of a sudden. No one had ever offered to take her shopping before.

"Hold that thought," she said and scurried off to the bedroom. She dug through her suitcase and found her sexiest underwear. She stripped off her unused diaper and t-shirt, sliding on a red lace thong and a silky black bra. With a quick check in the mirror to make sure her hair wasn't too crazy, she went back into the kitchen to find Micah cleaning off the table. When he saw her, he put down the plate he was holding and let out a low whistle, looking her up and down with admiration.

"Damn, baby girl. You're making me hungry all over again." She smiled and did a little twirl for him, letting him see the back view as well.

"Do you like it, Daddy?" she asked. He crossed the small kitchen and picked her up by her bum, carrying her towards the couch.

"How about I show you how much I like it," he growled. He sat down with her in his lap, pulling her legs apart so that she was straddling him. He pulled her down so that he could kiss her neck, letting his hands wander freely over her body. She sighed happily and closed her eyes as he lavished her with attention. He unhooked her bra, staring at her breasts with a hunger in his eyes. Her nipples hardened with arousal as he stared at her.

"Push them together for me, pumpkin." She held her breasts and pushed them up and in, presenting them to him. "Good girl. You look so perfect like that." He buried his face in her cleavage, kissing, licking, and sucking the skin of her breasts with passionate abandon. He gripped her buttocks as he devoured her, grinding her already wet pussy against him. Her happy sighs turned to moans as he smacked her ass, lightly at first, but then with increasing intensity.

"Do you like it when Daddy spanks you, little one?" he murmured against her nipple. She moaned and squirmed against him.

"Yes, Daddy. Spank my ass, please." He grinned up at her, and her stomach fluttered with excitement. She had already learned that that grin meant he had a dirty idea. So far, she had liked all of his dirty ideas.

"I'm so glad that you said that Princess." He pushed her face down onto the couch, swinging her legs so that she lay across his lap. With one hand he held down both of her wrists, and with the other, he rubbed her backside lovingly. She whined and squirmed, feeling herself go from wet to dripping almost instantly. He suddenly slapped her ass three times in a row, harder than he had before. She gasped and jerked at the sharp pain, gritting her teeth as she fought to take it like a good girl. He chuckled at her response and caressed her flesh tenderly with his fingertips.

"What do you think of that? Do you still like it when Daddy spanks you?" Her hips thrust back, her buttocks seeking more of the pleasure-pain and she nodded her head, silently asking for more.

"Use your words, kitten," he said sternly, popping her already tender buttcheeks playfully.

"Yes, Daddy," she gasped, overwhelmed by her burning desire. "I love you. Please, spank me more!" She hid her face in the pillows of the couch as he delivered blow after blow to her meaty buttocks. She squealed and squirmed as he increased the intensity, each blow landing harder than the last, but she made no move to stop him. The onslaught ceased, and he once again stroked her tender flesh. She peeked at him over her shoulder, his face was flushed, and he was breathing heavily, his eyes fixated on her bottom.

"Oh, sweetie, your little bum is so pink," he said quietly. His fingers on her backside felt so good, and once again, her hips rose, giving him access to all of her. He pushed aside her panties and began to lightly trace her cleft, tracing all the way down to the very center of her desire. He gently exploring her folds, holding her gaze with his own as he touched her.

"You're so wet, you dirty little thing. You must like getting spanked a lot. Daddy is going to have to come up with some other way to punish you." He twirled his fingertips around her sensitive nub, making her eyes roll back in her head. She was so overwhelmed with the sensation that she could neither squeal nor moan, only grip the pillows and writhe in his lap. Just as she thought that it couldn't get more intense, he once again brought his open hand down on her tender rear end. She cried out as she lost all sense of control, surrendering completely to his mastery over her body.

"You're not about to come, are you princess?" He smacked her twice in a row, painful smacks that made her jump and gasp. "Because I haven't given you permission to cum yet." He plunged a finger into her aching entrance, bringing her closer to a screaming climax. It took all of her willpower to hold back as he pumped his finger in and out of her, rubbing her g spot with every stroke.

"Please, Daddy, it feels so good. I want to cum so bad." He didn't seem convinced and spanked her hard, sending sparks of pain all through her. Her tender bottom was beginning to feel raw and bruised, and her body was screaming for release.

"I think you can do better than that, little one."

"Please, Daddy. I want to come on your hand so bad. I've been a good girl. Please let me cum. Your finger feels so good inside my slutty little pussy. Please, Daddy, can I?" He didn't answer her, only slid a second finger into her, stretching her out. She kicked her legs and squealed, feeling incredibly full and closer than ever to coming without permission.

"Daddy, please, I can't take it. Please let me come!"

"Yes princess, you can come for Daddy." He smacked her ass as he pumped his fingers into her, sending Lana over the edge. Her entire body shook as fingers drove into her relentlessly, drawing every ounce of pleasure that he could from her climax.

"That's it, kitten. Let it all out, all over Daddy's fingers. There's a good girl." He did not let up until she had stopped quivering and twitching in his lap, utterly spent. He rubbed her butt softly as she lay there, too worn out to move. She gave a shaky sigh as he removed his fingers and brought them to his mouth, licking them with a satisfied moan.

"Oh, baby girl, you are so sexy. You taste so sweet."

"Thank you, Daddy," she slurred, her words muffled by the couch cushions.

"So adorable," he chuckled and pulled her back up to sitting, cradling her in his lap. She wrapped her arms around his neck and rested her head on his shoulder, enjoying the feeling of being completely safe in his arms. After a few minutes, she came down from her euphoria to notice his erection poking into her bottom. She squirmed against it, eager to show him the same pleasure that he had just shown her. He gasped and moaned, the movement seemingly catching him off guard. She grinned as she reached her hand down between them, feeling his hard cock through his jeans.

"Oh kitten," he sighed, catching her lips with his and gently biting her lower lip. As their tongues intertwined, she undid his belt and pants. She got down on her knees on the floor in front of him as he brought out his cock, bouncing with excitement. As she wrapped her lips around him, she made a happy little moan.

"Did you like deepthroating me the other day, princess?" he asked as she slid him in and out of her mouth.

"Yes, Daddy." Her lips brushed the tip of his

cock as she spoke, sending a shiver through him.

"Do you want to practice that some more? See how far we can fit Daddy's cock down that pretty little throat?" She smiled up at him, turned on at the thought. He was so responsive. It was an absolute joy to bring him pleasure.

"Yes, Daddy, that sounds really fun." He put his hand on the back of her head, silently encouraging her to take him deep into her mouth. She worked his shaft deeper down her throat until she began to feel herself gag. Undeterred, she tried to fit even more of him down her throat, choking so hard that tears sprang to her eyes.

"Whoa, slow down, kitten. There's no rush. Just take it nice and slow." He caressed her cheek as she caught her breath. "Are you okay? Do you want to keep going?"

"Yes, Daddy," she said, taking him in her mouth again. He whispered encouragement to her as he thrust in and out of her throat, holding her face gently.

"That's better. Just relax, baby girl. Let

Daddy slide in and out. Good girl, just like that." She let herself relax into it, his hypnotic pace and soothing voice putting her into an almost zen-like state. The more she relaxed, the deeper he pumped into her throat, and the better it felt. She could feel some drool begin to dribble out of her mouth and down his shaft, but she was so drunk on lust that she didn't care.

"Yeah, take Daddy's cock just like that, princess. You're doing so good. I love it when you drool on my cock, baby." She let a little more dribble out just to see the delighted expression on his face. "Daddy's dirty girl. You're going to make me cum, sweetheart." She caressed his balls, wordless encouragement for him to come in her mouth again. He had other plans, however, and grabbed her by her hair, pulling her off his shaft and standing so that he was looming over her. He worked his cock furiously over her open mouth and let loose all over her face and breasts. It was sensual and erotic, the way his hot seed rained down over her, and she caught as much as she could in her mouth, savoring the taste of him. He sat back down with a sigh, still gripping her tightly by the hair. He brought her face to his, kissing her deeply as his ragged breath came back down to normal.

"Oh, sweetheart, you're so sexy. You look so pretty covered in my cum."

"Thank you, Daddy," she said, glowing at the compliment. Indeed, she did feel pretty and sexy around him. He had a way of making sex not only satisfying but really fun and intimate as well. She felt so lucky as he bundled her up in his arms and carried her off to the bathroom.

He drew a bubble bath for her, stripping off her little red thong and holding her hand as she got it. The warm water felt amazing, and Micah's large hands began to massage her scalp, sending her even further into relaxed bliss. He scrubbed her skin clean with a loofah, taking extra care to be gentle on her tender and bruised bottom. Lana found that she rather liked the marks left by him. She loved having a tangible reminder of pleasure they had shared together and how it marked her as his. He washed her hair, rinsing out the suds with some water from a plastic cup. She leaned back, letting the warm water cascade over her hair. Once she was all clean, he spent a while rubbing her shoulders, letting her relax in the warm water while he eased any remaining tension away. Eventually, he let out the water and bundled her body and hair into towels before carrying her to bed.

"I'm not sleepy, Daddy," she said as he lowered her onto the mattress.

"Neither am I, kitten. Our night together is just getting started." He kissed her hungrily as he began to unwrap the towel from around her naked body.

Chapter 12

They slept in late the next morning, both of them were exhausted from a long night of lovemaking. Micah made pancakes while Lana packed an overnight bag. One quick stop by his hunting cabin to make sure it was locked and secure and they were on the road to Atlanta. He played some country music tunes on their way, and Lana took turns enjoying the scenery and snoozing in the passenger seat. It wasn't a very far trip, and before she knew it, they were in the city. They stopped by his apartment first to drop off their bags and freshen up after the trip. He lived in a high rise apartment in the downtown area of the city. The inside was nice, with industrial decor. Lana wouldn't be surprised if he had hired a professional decorator.

Once they were settled and unpacked, he took her

to a small boutique nearby and bought her a few dresses and a couple of shoes. She offered to pay for them herself, but he refused.

"I know how little office staff make. You hold onto your money, let me take care of it." He winked at her as he handed over his card to the cashier. "I was thinking that we could have some lunch and then afterward there is another shop I want to take you to."

"More dresses? Honestly, I think I have enough for now."

"No little one, not more dresses." He hadn't elaborated any further, leaving Lana to wonder. They ate at a small restaurant nearby, Lana having soup and salad and Micah having a Reuben sandwich. She wondered where he was going to take her next but didn't pester him about it, wanting it to be a surprise. Her time with him had taught her to appreciate how much sweeter a little bit of mystery and anticipation can make things.

It turned out to be a lingerie shop but one unlike

any that she had ever seen before. Upon their arrival, they were greeted by a personal shopper who offered them champagne. She took Lana's measurements and brought out a few samples for Lana to try on. Micah told her to take her time and to pick out whatever she liked.

"I'm sure whatever you choose will be lovely. I have some things I want to look at myself." Lana didn't have much experience with lingerie and relied on the shopper's opinion to make her decisions. She finally settled on three items that she thought Micah would enjoy and met him back out front. He had already rung up his items, wrapped and tucked away in bags so that she couldn't see them. More surprises.

Back at his place, he said that he wanted to take her someplace nice for dinner and that she should put on one of her pretty new dresses with something sexy underneath. After her shower, she picked out a black sheer bodysuit to wear underneath a purple form-fitting dress that hit just above the knee. She did her hair and makeup especially nice, happy to have a reason to wear a smokey eye for once. As she came out from the bathroom, Micah looked very happy to see her. His face lit up like a kid on Christmas morning.

"Oooh baby girl, you look good enough to eat. Come here." Lana giggled and came close to him. He held a box in his hand which he handed to her. "I have something to add to your beautiful ensemble." She opened the box to find a vibrator that was shaped like a large U so that it stimulated both the g-spot and clitoris.

"You want me to wear this during dinner?" she asked, confused.

"I do. I have the controls installed on my phone. You are mine, and I want to be able to play with you whenever and wherever I wish. Is that understood?" She flushed, her breath quickening with the thought. A dirty little secret that only the two of them knew about.

"Yes, Daddy," she whispered, nearly breathless with excitement.

"Let's see you putting it in, kitten." She smiled and reached under her skirt, unclasping the bodysuit at the crotch. Maintaining eye contact with him, she licked her fingers and slid them over her pussy and the vibe, giving it a little extra slip before sliding the vibe in. Once it was snugly in place, she snapped her bodysuit back into place. It felt strange between her legs yet not uncomfortable.

"Good girl. Now, let's try this out." He took out his phone and tapped the screen a few times. She felt a powerful vibration between her legs, making her legs quiver. A little squeak escaped her lips as she tried to maintain her composure. It hit both of her most sensitive areas at once, making it impossible to think, speak, or walk. He watched her intently, letting the vibrator go on for several seconds before stopping it with a few more taps on his phone.

"Goodness, how high did you have that up?" she said, trying to regain her breath.

"That was the lowest setting, little one." He

put his arm around her waist, pulling her close to him. She shivered as he brushed a strand of hair out of her face and looked her in the eye. "Now, since I'm a very generous man, I'm going to go ahead and give you permission to cum as many times as you need to, pumpkin." She flushed at the thought of climaxing in public and wondered how she would even pull that off. She was certain that she would look as though she were having some sort of fit. Given the strength of the lowest setting, she didn't think she would be able to stop herself from cumming, however, especially now that she knew that was his goal.

"Thank you, Daddy," she said, smiling up at him with adoration. She marveled at his ability to both keep her interested and keep her wanting more. He said they would walk to dinner, that the restaurant was nearby. With every step she took, she could feel the vibe moving between her legs, the subtle stimulation maker her wetter and wetter with every step. She was also filled with anticipation, wondering when he would turn it on and begin her sweet torture. When they arrived at the restaurant less than ten minutes later, he had not yet turned it on, and suspense was killing her. He didn't turn it on until the waiter came over to drop off the bread and take their drink orders. Micah had his phone out on the table, with the app up and ready to go. As soon as Lana opened her mouth to say that she would have water to drink, she felt the vibe come to life between her legs and her words were cut short by a choked cry that she covered up somewhat convincingly with a cough.

"The lady will have a white wine, and I will have a lager. Thank you very much." As the waiter nodded and walked off, he turned the vibe back off again. "Cat got your tongue there, kitten?" He looked very pleased with himself. She started to reply but again, her words were cut short as the vibe came back, even stronger than before. *This must be level two.* She clenched the table cloth as the strong sensation had her immediately on the verge of an orgasm. Micah took her hand, letting her grip his fingers as hard as she needed to maintain a straight face. Just as she thought she was going to climax in front of all the people sitting around them, he suddenly turned the vibe off again. She sat there panting, feeling her pussy twitch around the vibe, seeking the orgasm it had been building up to. The waiter returned, setting the drinks down on the table.

"Will you need another minute to look at the menu?" Just as the waiter turned his attention to Lana, looking at her expectantly, the vibe came back to life.

"I, I, I," Lana stuttered as if her brain had suddenly been turned off, which is exactly how she felt as her climax came roaring back. She managed to hold it off through sheer willpower alone.

"I think we'll need another minute," Micah interjected and smiled disarmingly at the waiter.

"Ok," he said. "My name is Keith if either of you has any questions." He gave Lana a somewhat quizzical look as he left, but Lana was so lost in her ecstasy that she barely noticed. Micah leaned forward, whispering so that only she could hear.

"Don't hold back, princess. Daddy already told you that you can come as many times as you need to tonight. I know you want to. Go on, let it out." She couldn't hold it in anymore. As her climax shook her body, she bit the palm of her hand, muffling her quiet whimpers as best as she could.

"Good girl. One more, then we can pick what we want to eat for tonight." She looked at him wide-eyed, unable to say a word as he turned the vibe up the third level. Her first orgasm had barely finished when a second one came crashing over her. She was visibly shaking, her eyes rolling back in her head as she twitched and tried not to make any noise. Just when she thought she might lose her mind, lost forever in a swirling vortex of pleasure, he turned the vibe back off. Micah looked at her with a smirk as she sighed and closed her eyes, recovering from her ordeal. He opened his menu and perused it for a moment.

"I think I might have a nice cut of steak tonight, what about you, honey?" he said, his voice dripping with sweetness and innocence. She couldn't answer yet. She was still coming down from the intense sensations he had inflicted on her. It was looking more and more like Micah might be the death of her and she wasn't entirely sure that she minded. With a shaky hand she picked up her menu but the words were a blur. She tried to focus but her mind was still reeling from her orgasms.

"Daddy, you pick something," she said, sighing in defeat. She put the menu down and sat back, closing her eyes.

"Aww, is my baby girl too cum drunk to think straight?" She nodded, too dazed to even be embarrassed. She wasn't sure if she could take it anymore. On the other hand, she wasn't sure that she wanted him to stop, either. She looked around the room, wondering if anyone had noticed or cared about her little "fit." She saw couples and groups of friends all around her, laughing, talking, and eating their meals. The idea that they might look over at any second and see Micah controlling her body was exhilarating. She wanted everyone to know that she was his, and he was hers.

"How does pumpkin ravioli sound, sweetie?" he said sweetly. She braced herself, expecting him to turn the vibe back on as soon as she answered.

"Yes, that sounds delicious." She managed to get out the whole sentence without him triggering the vibe, and she actually found herself missing it.

What is he turning me into? She thought with a smile. He made her feel so wanton and insatiable. Just when she thought she'd had too much, he proved that she hadn't had nearly enough. Micah signaled to the waiter that they were ready to order. As soon as the waiter arrived at their table, the vibe came back to life. Lana's eyes crossed slightly, but she managed to keep a straight face otherwise. Her pussy was incredibly sensitive after her orgasms, but he kept it on the low setting, keeping her warmed up.

"Yes, I was wondering what kinds of seasonings you use on your steaks?" Micah asked the waiter. As the man began to answer, Micah made a subtle movement, and the vibe suddenly started pulsing on and off in an undulating pattern. Their conversation suddenly seemed distant and hazy. As her eyes fluttered closed, the pulse got stronger, keeping the same steady pace.

"My date here is interested in the pumpkin ravioli, but she was wondering if it has any dairy in it," she heard Micah say. He seemed to be deliberately asking unnecessary questions in order to make her cum in front of the waiter. *So evil,* she thought as she gripped the tablecloth and tried not to look like an insane person.

"What do you think, honey. Would you like the ravioli?" He looked at her with fake innocence all over his face, his sea-green eyes twinkling mischievously.

"Mm-hmm," she nodded, and the waiter jotted down her order. He was about to walk off before Micah stopped him, turning the vibe up to the third level, keeping the pulse pattern going. Lana audibly sighed but managed to keep a straight face otherwise. She gripped her legs together, trying to maintain control.

"I was thinking about maybe trying the chicken, what do you recommend?" he asked the waiter, discreetly reprogramming the vibe. He eliminated the pulse, keeping it strong but steady. She wouldn't be able to hold back an orgasm if he kept this up for long. The waiter prattled on about the advantages of one dish over another and Lana could feel her orgasm building, knew it would be long before it came crashing over her and she would be powerless to stop it. Just as she was about to cum, he cut the vibe off. She was left trembling, out of breath, and desperately clenching around the dead vibe, seeking the stimulation that had just been ripped away from her. She glared at him but he pretended not to notice as he handed his menu back to the waiter.

"You know, I think I'll have the steak after all. Thanks so much." He turned back to Lana, grinning like the cat that ate the canary.

"You're so mean," she pouted. Her

breathing was hard as she was still recovering from the intense experience.

"Why would you even say that?" he asked with a fake shocked expression on his face.

"We're having such a lovely evening." She started to reply, but her response was cut short when he turned the vibe back on full force. Before she could even form a thought, she was already cumming again. Her eyes rolled back, and her legs flailed, kicking him under the table. The effort to not make noise was so great that she had to bang on the table a little and hope that people thought that she was laughing. Or killing a bug. She didn't really care anymore, and evidently neither did Micah. He was laughing now and rubbing the sore spot on his shin where she had kicked him.

"I guess I deserved that," he said as he turned the vibe off. Lana relaxed back against her chair, utterly spent. "Had enough, pumpkin?" Lana nodded, still unable to speak. He chuckled and nodded, patting her hand.

"Okay, okay. Daddy will leave you alone for

the rest of dinner. You can relax." Lana took a sip of her wine to soothe her parched throat and steady herself.

True to his word, Micah did not activate her vibe again for the rest of dinner. She scarfed down her ravioli, partially because she was ravenous after cumming so many times and partially because it was incredibly delicious. She was so distracted by the vibrator that she didn't really notice until now how fancy the restaurant he had taken her to was at first. Now that the food was out, however, she was starting to appreciate it more. They ordered dessert, a slice of chocolate cake to share. It was every bit as delicious as the entree had been.

"I can't believe this place is in walking distance to your apartment," she said, taking the last bite of cake. "You must eat here all the time!"

"I did at first but to be honest, these days I just order in from somewhere. I have had a dinner companion as lovely as you in quite some time, and I hate eating alone." She blushed at the compliment and put her fork down.

"Boy, I'm stuffed. As good as that was, I don't think I could eat another bite."

"I'll get the check. Then we can head back to my place." The thought of curling up in Micah's arms and going to sleep sounded really nice. However, something told her he wasn't in the mood for sleep. This suspicion was confirmed when the vibe came back to life when the waiter brought the check. Even on the low setting, it made Lana's eyebrows shoot up and her breath quicken.

"Just a second, if you don't mind," he said to the waiter before he could walk away again.

"I just want to make sure that everything is correct." He pretended to look over the check, but really he was only turning her vibe up another level. Lana had to close her eyes and turn her face down toward her lap to keep from giving the whole thing away. After several long, excruciating seconds, Micah finally handed the check and his card to the waiter.

"Everything looks perfect. Thank you so

much for your patience," he said, giving the man a big smile. He turned back to Lana and smirked. "You have until the waiter to comes back to cum one last time and that will be your last chance for the evening." He turned the vibe up to the third level and watched her face contort, knowing that it would take almost no time at all with the vibes that powerful. Sure enough, her eyes were soon rolling back in her head and she bit her palm again as her body subtly trembled. A tear escaped her eye from the force of her own bite and the force of her orgasm. A low moan escaped her lips but it was too quiet for anyone else but Micah to hear. Micah turned the vibe off as the waiter returned with their check. He signed it with a flourish, being extra generous with the tip just in case the man had noticed anything strange about their dinner out. Lana got up with shaky legs, gratefully taking Micah's arm as he led her out of the restaurant, both of them going slowly until she could regain her footing.

Back at his place, he was on her within seconds of walking in the door. He pushed her roughly over the arm of the couch, forcing her ass in the air and her face down into the cushions. He ripped open the bodysuit and pulled out the vibe, making her moan slightly at the sensation.

"Oh, baby girl, you are so wet right now. You came so hard, didn't you my dirty girl?" She could hear his pants unzipping, and within moments he was inside of her.

"Remember what I said back at the restaurant, no more cumming for the rest of the night." He pumped into her furiously, stroking her butthole with his thumb as he pounded her pussy. He didn't last long, all that teasing back at the restaurant had clearly had an effect on him. He grabbed the flesh of her buttocks as he drove himself deeper inside of her and let loose all the cum that had been building up all evening. It felt so warm and delicious inside of her that she wanted to climax again. She loved the way it felt to be full of his cock and his cum, but she held herself back, priding herself on being a good girl for Daddy. He finally stopped shuddering and twitching inside of her and pulled out, his warm jizz dripping out of her. He sat on the couch and pulled her onto his lap, burying his face in her neck with a shaky sigh. She wrapped her arms around his neck, feeling shaky, exhausted, and completely happy.

"I'm so glad I found you," he whispered, holding her tighter still. "I can't believe how lucky I am, how perfect you are." She smiled dreamily. She had just been thinking the same thing about him.

"So are you, Daddy," she said. They complimented one another so well. She felt certain that fate must have brought them together somehow. As he pulled her face to his for a kiss, she hoped that fate would allow her to keep him, her perfect Daddy.

Chapter 13

Lana navigated her hybrid through the narrow mountain roads. She had grown more accustomed to driving on these steep dirt paths over the past few months, but it still made her nervous. She preferred to let Micah drive when she could, but he wouldn't be able to meet her until later that evening. He had given her the key to his hunting cabin when he saw her last, at Thanksgiving, and asked her if she would spend her Christmas break with him. She had said yes immediately, as if it were even a question. They had spent every moment together that they could over these past few months, visiting each other on holidays, long weekends, even playing hooky a few times in Micah's case. They texted each other and Skyped as much as possible as well, enjoying each other's company just as much as they enjoyed fucking each other. After all of these months together, their passion had not cooled down one little bit. He would often ask her to sneak off to the bathroom to take a sexy picture of herself to send to him. She loved showing off her body to him at every opportunity, never getting tired of how sexy it made her feel. All of the teasing made it so much hotter when they were finally able to get together to relieve the tension. She was looking forward to relieving some of that tension now. Thanksgiving had been fun, but there had been too many family obligations and food comas to fully enjoy one another to the extent that they usually did. That's why they decided to go away for the Christmas break. It was going to be just the two of them for a full week and Lana had been looking forward to this very much.

Micah had to finish up some work stuff before he would be totally free so he had told her to just head straight for the cabin, and he would meet her there later. He gave her a very specific list of instructions to follow once she arrived at the cabin. She loved it when he did that. It could turn the most boring, mundane task into a sexy game. She pulled into the cabin, activating the flashlight on her phone to see in the dark. Letting herself in, she turned on all of the lights and the heat. As she made the place ready, she could feel herself already getting wet, every boring detail suddenly becoming an act of foreplay just because he had ordered her to do it. She lit candles all over the living room, dimmed the lights, and put on the playlist that he had sent to her. Once the cabin had heated up, she stripped off her clothes and hung them carefully in the closet. He liked it when she was neat and tidy, calling her his domesticated little fuckslave. That never failed to make her pussy throb. From her bag, she pulled out the collar that he had bought for her with a heart-shaped lock on the front. Once she put it on, only he had the key to free her again. She fully expected to wear it for the entirety of their stay. Next, she put on a pair of thigh-high stockings, the only clothing that she would be permitted to wear over the next week. The silky material felt wonderful against her bare skin, and she imagined that it was Micah's hand sliding up her legs instead. She checked the time anxiously. It wouldn't be long now. The final touch was a butt plug with a cute furry tail attached. Lana had seen it online and fell in love. Micah had bought it for her as an early Christmas present, having it shipped to her house so that she could wear it this evening. She applied a small amount of lube and slid it in with a quiet squeak. It felt nice, but it would have felt even better if Micah had been the one to slide it in. He would have teased her with it, making her beg for it before finally pushing it in. He knew exactly how to reduce her to a whimpering, horny mess. Once it was in, she checked herself out in the mirror, giving it a little shake. The furry tail danced from side to side, and she giggled. It was every bit as cute as she hoped it would be and the sensations it made as the tail swayed back and forth were very stimulating.

It was almost time for his arrival. She went to the living room and knelt in the middle of the floor, waiting. She kept her knees splayed wide, making sure that he would have full access to every part of her. Her hands were behind her back so that she wouldn't grab for his cock or her clit without permission. He had learned that one of the only effective punishments was to deny her orgasms. Everything else only turned her on and encouraged bad behavior. Denying her the ability to cum, however, kept her in line. A few days without getting off and she became a whiny, needy little thing, willing to comply with whatever he asked of her to be able to cum again. Tonight, he had given her permission to cum as many times as she liked. They had barely gotten to fuck over Thanksgiving, and he said that he wanted to make up for the lost time. However, if she disobeyed him or broke any of the rules, that privilege could be revoked at any time, so she had to be on her best behavior. As she waited, she could feel her skin tingle in anticipation, her pussy already drooling down her legs. At last, she saw his headlights on the wall as he pulled in. As he came inside, her heart leaped with joy. It was finally time.

"Hello, kitten," he said, grinning at her as he took off his coat and put his keys on the hook by the door. He came over to where she knelt, inspecting her from all angles. "Well, don't you look lovely this evening? I love your new tail." He pulled on it lightly, just enough to make her gasp. Then, he kissed her long and deep. She stayed on her knees, mindful that he had not ordered her otherwise just yet, and strained herself upwards to meet his kiss. He broke off the kiss, pushed her gently back down to sit on her heels. As he looked down at her, she noticed that he was still in his suit and the dichotomy of him being fully clothed as she knelt before him, naked and fully on display was deeply erotic. She could his erection already bulging in his pants and licked her lips hungrily. He saw the way she was looking at him and smirked.

"Already hungry for Daddy's cock, little one?" He rubbed it through his pants, teasing her.

"Yes, Daddy. I'm so hungry for your cock. Please, can I taste it?" She looked up at him with her best puppy dog eyes, pleading. He took her by the back of the head and pulled her face to his crotch, rubbing it against his hard cock through the soft fabric of her pants. She moaned as he rubbed himself on her, wanting to taste him all the more as she felt how hard he already was for her. He grabbed her by the hair, forcing her head back so that she was looking up at him. He stroked her face lovingly with the back of his hand as he gazed down at her.

"Unzip my pants, little one," he instructed. She took her hands from behind her back, lowering his zipper slowly while looking up at him. He reached down and freed his erection from her pants, chuckling as the wide eyed expression of glee she got when she saw it.

"Stroke it." She ran her hands up and down the length of him, longing to take him deep down her throat. His hands in her hair kept her firmly in place however and she had to make do with touching it for now. She knew that if she was a good girl for him, her patience would be rewarded.

"Oh baby girl, I've been thinking about this for so long." He took off his belt as she stroked him and let his pants drop. "I've been thinking about your tight little holes and how I'm going to fuck every last one of them. What do you think of that?" She shivered, his dirty words inflaming her desire further.

"Oh, Daddy, yes. Please fuck all of my holes. I need your cock so badly." He smiled and stepped out of his pants, kicking off his shoes.

"Open," he said, and automatically she opened her mouth as wide as she could. He had trained her well over the past few months, and she responded to his commands eagerly and without hesitation. He laid his balls in her mouth, stroking himself slowly as she licked and slurped at him, moaning with excitement.

"That's it, good girl." Finally, he let her taste

his cock, sliding it into her mouth, slowly at first but plunging it deeper and faster with every stroke. He had trained her throat as well, and she could swallow his cock whole without batting an eye now. She was very proud of her deep-throating abilities, loving the way he used her mouth for his pleasure.

"Do you like it when Daddy fucks your pretty little face?" he asked. He loved asking her questions when she had a mouth full of his cock, often saying that she looked "adorable" when she tried to answer him. She made a muffled "yes" noise as he plunged deeper down her throat, moaning with satisfaction.

"Do you want to touch your drippy little pussy?" he asked, continuing to fuck her throat. Again, she answered "yes" as best as she could with his cock lodged in her throat. She didn't move her hand to her pussy just yet. She had learned the hard way that asking her if she wanted something was not the same as giving her permission to do it. He pulled her off of his cock by her hair, letting her gasp for air for a moment, drool dripping from her lips. He looked at her for a moment, enjoying the sight of her as she knelt before him, naked and so eager to please. He plunged back into her throat before finally giving her permission to touch herself. She rubbed at her clit furiously as she choked on his cock, loving the way it intensified every sensation. He groped her tits, pinching the nipples hard as he pumped in and out of her mouth. As he grabbed the back of her head, pushing himself balls deep into her mouth, she came forcefully, her legs jerking underneath her as she finally released the tension that had been building for so long.

"That's it, princess. Good girl," he said as he noticed that she was climaxing. He held her down on his cock until she stopped gyrating, then pulled her up for air. He let her take in a gasp before plunging his tongue in her mouth, tasting her sweet mouth. "Oh, how I've missed you little one." He pushed her back onto her heels, taking his shirt off so that he was now completely naked. He sat down on the couch and started casually stroking his cock as he stared at her.

"Get on all fours," he told her, grinning as she obeyed quickly. "What a good slut. Now turn around and let Daddy see your new tail." She maneuvered herself so that her ass was facing him, letting him get a better look at the butt plug.

"Oh princess, you look so pretty. Do you feel pretty?" She shook her tail and giggled.

"Yes, Daddy, I feel really pretty. Thank you so much for my present."

"You're welcome, baby girl. Now get over here and ride Daddy's cock." She stayed on her hands and knees, knowing how much he liked the way she looked when she crawled towards him. She climbed up onto the couch, straddling him. Her pussy was soaking wet after her orgasm, and he slipped inside of her easily.

"Oh kitten, you're so fucking tight," he growled as he grabbed her hips, holding her down onto his cock. Sometimes, when they were apart, Lana would forget just how big his cock was. As he split her open, stretching her pussy around his thickness, she found herself having to move slowly until she could adjust to his girth. He grabbed her by the face and kissed her deeply, letting her do all the work as she gripped him with her tight pussy. She loved the way he kissed her, slowly and sensually exploring her mouth. She impaled herself on him again and again, loving the way he filled her up.

"Daddy, I missed you so much," she whispered as she slid up and down on him, letting her head fall back in ecstasy. She reached down and touched her clit, working her way toward another orgasm. As she got closer, he began to pump his hips, driving his cock up into her hard and fast. She cried out as she came again, her thighs quivering around him as her eyes rolled back. He let himself go as well, flooding her pussy with his cum as she clenched around him. He pulled her back to him for a kiss, a long slow kiss that contained all of the passion they had been forced by distance to hold back. It felt so good to be in his arms again, to feel him inside of her again. She felt that she had found the place that she belonged with him. They kissed for so long that she felt him begin to get hard again inside of her. Micah had the quickest turnaround time of any man she had ever met. He claimed that it was due entirely to her sexiness, saying that it was only because she drove him so wild. He picked her up, carrying her to the bedroom with her legs wrapped around him, his cock still deep inside of her. They fell onto the bed together, Lana underneath him as they resumed their kiss. She let her fingers run through his silky black hair as their tongues intertwined, and he began to slowly pump himself in and out of her. At last, he was giving her the long slow fucking that they had both been longing for. He put her hand on her clit as he filled her.

"I want you to cum on my cock again, baby girl," he said. He took her nipple in her mouth as she began to rub her button, moaning and squirming beneath him. She spread her legs wider, eager to take him still deeper inside of her. No matter how many time they fucked, it was never enough. He was her sweetest addiction, just as she was his. She let her orgasm build slowly this time, enjoying the feeling of his hands and mouth on her, the feeling of his weight on her, memorizing every detail. She held herself back, wanting to ride the edge as long as possible until she could hold back no longer. She came with a strangled cry, digging her nails into his back as the ecstasy took her.

"Good girl. That's Daddy's good little slut. You're doing so good sweetheart, but Daddy isn't done with you yet." He pulled out, watching with delight as his cum leaked out of her. He maneuvered the butt plug in and out of her, letting his cum and hers lubricate her rear entrance.

"Get on all fours," he commanded. "Daddy wants that ass next." She rolled over, getting up onto her hands and knees. She felt him slide the plug out and place his cock there instead. Slowly, gently, he penetrated her, rubbing her clit as she adjusted to his girth.

"Does that feel good, sweetheart?" he whispered in her ear. She gasped and moaned, struggling to speak through the haze of lust.

"Y-yes Daddy, that is so good. Please fuck my ass, please, please." She was already close to cumming again. She had learned that anal stimulation was a big turn on for her, one of the many things that she had learned about herself since meeting Micah.

"That's it, princess, take that cock." His dirty words pushed her over the edge, and this time as she came, she screamed. So many orgasms so close in a row were bringing her dangerously close to being overstimulated into a whiny, crying mess. As he pumped into her ass even harder, she knew that she would be in that state in very shortly. It was going to be a very long night.

Chapter 14

On Christmas morning, they got up early, excited to exchange gifts. Micah put on a pot of coffee while Lana started a fire. They gave each other their carefully wrapped packages and then tore the wrapping off at the same time. Lana had given Micah a book, the newest in a fantasy series that he was a fan of. Micah had given Lana a box, which she shook curiously.

"Well, go on, open it," he said impatiently. She grinned and took the lid off to see a key laying inside.

"What's this for," she asked, crinkling her brow in confusion.

"It's a key to my apartment. I want you to move in with me, Lana." She looked at him in shock, totally blindsided by the question. "I've already spoken with a friend of mine who works for the Board of Education. He said that they're always in need of good office staff in Atlanta and he can put in a good word for you. What do you think?" She considered it for a moment, wondering what it would be like to be with him all the time, to not have to spend so much time on planes, in cars, on the phone. There was very little keeping her in Jacksonville. She nodded, deciding.

"Okay, I will. I'll move in with you." He let out a whoop of excitement and tackled her, wrapping her up in a bear hug.

"When? When?" he asked excitedly, peppering her forehead with kisses.

"At the end of the year," she giggled, tickled by his excitement. "Let me finish out the year, that will give us plenty of time to make all the necessary arrangements."

"Okay," he grinned. "I suppose I can wait that long." He kissed her, long and deep, then looked her in the eyes.

"I love you, Lana," he said, suddenly very seriously. "I'm so lucky to have you. I don't know what I'd do without you." She grinned, her heart beaming with a happiness beyond anything she had ever felt before.

"I love you too, Daddy. We're both lucky. I don't know what I would do without you either and now we don't ever have to find out."

Who is Tina Moore?

Tina Moore has enjoyed the lifestyle of a Mommy Domme for several years. She began exploring kink and BDSM in her youth and found her love of being a strict Mommy Domme in early 2000. Tina Moore is now an author of many MDLG, DDLG and ABDL themed novels.

Follow her on:

Author Page on Amazon

Instagram @tinamoore.kdp

If you enjoyed this book, it would be much appreciated if you leave **a review on Amazon**.

www.ingramcontent.com/pod-product-compliance
Lightning Source LLC
Chambersburg PA
CBHW031020190726
48286CB00003BA/944